Cyril Dabydeen

THE WIZARD SWAMI

Peepal Tree Press

First published in Great Britain in 1989
Peepal Tree Press
53, Grove Farm Crescent
Yorkshire
England

ISBN 0 94833 19 X

'In the end it [El Dorado] drew him out of the Tower of London, which was his perfect setting, perhaps unconsciously sought, where, liberated from his inadequacy in the role the age imposed on him, he [Ralegh] reached that stillness where the fact of life and action was reconciled with the fact of death. This was what he had plundered, this latecoming to the quest that destroyed so many.'

V.S. Naipaul, *The Loss Of Eldorado*

Chapter One

Devan slowly postured himself, folding his legs Buddha-style. Then, closing his eyes, he concentrated with all his power. Suddenly he imagined the houses in the village moving, houses with legs walking away. Astonished, he opened his eyes at once, got up, and rushed to the window. He saw the houses as they always were, standing on stilts, the green grass scattered about in desultory fashion, hibiscus brush unevenly forming the hedges with red flowers hanging pendulant and some waywardly protruding, vying for sunlight. Sighing with relief, he inhaled the scent of jasmine which remained in his nostrils for a while, and sucked more air into his lungs as he recalled the image of the houses moving, walking away as if they would leave the coastland forever and head towards the sea. He rubbed his eyes, still horrified. Then, somewhat reluctantly, he walked back to his room and, taking his time, postured his five-foot-six frame once more, closed his eyes and began meditating again, though now a little nervously. Nothing happened; he concentrated harder but the houses remained where they were, steadfast on their stilts. A mild sensation of darkness came upon him as he concentrated harder, and yet nothing happened. In a fury he got up and stomped about the room. 'Blast!' he cried. 'Blast!'

Tara, his wife, who'd been peeping at his antics all along through the key hole, moaned. What was the matter with Devan? Why didn't he behave like other husbands? Why didn't he go out and work and earn money like everyone else? She grimaced as she watched him stomping about, his lips pursed. Yes, why did he keep meditating all the time, believing he had a mission in life? 'Is me destiny,' he'd told her last night and every other night for the past two weeks, and even though she'd scoffed at him he continued repeating this. Now she was really fed-up with hearing all his talk about Hinduism. Again she watched him, his eyes rolling about his head, wringing his hands in dismay, the large volumes scattered about him. Hadn't she hidden the books for a while? But it was no use: Devan was adept at finding them again in the small house his father had built for them from his meagre savings. She shook her head sadly as he folded his legs Buddha-style once more, closing his eyes to meditate, muttering to himself. But when his face broke into a smile, his expression one of peace, it was too much for Tara.

Pushing the door open, she charged loudly: 'What yuh studyin' for, Devan? Tell me dat!' Sensing trouble, Devan closed his eyes firmly and mentally prepared himself for what was coming, and Tara repeated the charges, her hands akimbo. 'Yes, what yuh studyin', eh?'

'Indian history,' he muttered, eyes still closed.

'Indian what?' she pretended not to hear.

'You deaf or what, woman?' he let out, exasperated, eyes opening widely and looking at her as if he was seeing her for the first time.

Tara, undaunted, started the questioning all over again, her small frame shaking, her bust throbbing, and Devan closed his eyes again. His stillness infuriated her. 'Yes, what you studyin' eh?' Tara's voice drummed in his ears.

'Indian culture,' he muttered, and opened his eyes, focusing on the book before him. Then he smiled, confusing Tara who blinked rapidly; she could not read – even in English – and the spidery-looking Hindi alphabets appeared bewildering to her. She moaned again, her anger and frustration mounting, and let out: 'Why you not study how to get money instead? You tink is culture goin' to mine de children?'

This piqued Devan immensely, yet he forced his attention on the Hindi words, thinking that maybe God had cursed him in giving him such a wife. He sighed three or four times in quick succession. But nothing could stop Tara now: she fumed and fretted, harangued and mocked in an unending tirade. Devan felt this was his greatest test and, closing his eyes once more, the Hindi words still on his mind, he retreated into an impregnable mental state. Again he smiled.

But Tara's shrill voice began to break through the barrier as she attacked him for his laziness, heartlessness, and cruelty.

'You do nutten all day!' she fired. 'You only pray an' meditate. For what? You leave me to do all de work, to go to rice field an' slave. Tell me, Devan, is dat why you marry me, eh? Fo' me to mek children an' slave while you go act like sadhu. Only mad people does do dat!'

Once more Devan sighed, forcing himself to think of God, the One Creator of the Universe, the Supreme Consciousness... he mouthed the words... the Omniscient, Omnipresent Being. But Tara continued, undaunted: 'I go have to mine de children! I go have to tek care of everything at home! What kind o' husband is you, eh? Tell me dat!' She had almost exhausted herself as she stood closer before him, breathing in hard, her small hands fluttering at her waist because of the exertion.

As if unable to bear it any longer, Devan put his little fingers to his ears. Tara's voice faded; it was as if she was walking away from him, though not far, unlike the houses. 'Ah, blessed fingers,' he murmured, a wide smile sweeping across his face. 'Blessed state.'

An hour later Tara said to Devan, 'I go leave you now.'

Devan pretended not to hear. She'd said this many times before, without ever carrying out her threat, yet he watched her outside the room, the way her lips tightened. 'Mark my words, Devan; I go leave an' never return.' No, she wouldn't carry out her threat.

Serenely he asked, 'Leaving?'

'Yes-yes, man!' she snapped, and hurried to pack her things. Even as Devan listened to her tumbling clothes and drawers about, he was still convinced she wouldn't leave. And when he looked out of the window he seemed to be unaware that Tara was gathering the children and stepping out.

Only when the house was really quiet did he suddenly feel the absence. 'Tara,' he called out from his room. Then he called out for his son Jotish; he wanted him to gather hibiscus flowers from the neighbour's hedge and to sit close to him so he could start teaching him about Hinduism. No answer; the house was still, save for his own breathing. He inhaled, breathing harder. 'Jotish,' he called again, more loudly this time. He didn't care so much for his daughters, Shanti and Devi; they were solely their mother's concern. Again he called out for Tara; the house was deathly still. He got up quickly and searched every part of the house; next, he looked out of the window down the main road, imagining Tara dragging their son along with her wherever she had gone; and the girls too. He moaned again and muttered, 'Ah, she really lef' me for good this time.'

But later, for a while, Devan felt happy at his new freedom; now he could meditate and pray as long as he wished in absolute silence. He read from the *Bhagavad Gita* diligently, an hour each day, then from the *Ramayana*, then closed his eyes and reflected on the Supreme Being. In such a serene mental state, a smile would break from his lips. He imagined Jotish close to him, then Tara: she too meditating. But he opened his eyes immediately, because this was an impossibility.

Yet, more than ever he was sure that he had a mission to fulfil. Now, he had to pray and meditate and pursue goodness and truth; later, his appointed task, and perhaps his rewards, would be determined. He felt even more serene.

But when he grew cramped from sitting in one position and opened his eyes, he saw the bare walls of his room, the wood peeling in parts. He willed this image to disappear. Unconsciously, he waited to hear Tara's voice; he was used to her being around, he said to himself; she shouldn't have left, and he realised just then how much he really missed her. Now he would have to do all the housekeeping, which would keep him from praying and meditating. Then he chided himself, 'Habit, habit. I mus' break dis habit.'

Later, as the loneliness grew upon him, he muttered to himself, 'Is it really true she lef'?' But a line from the *Mahabharata* floated into his thoughts, and in his anxiety he repeated: 'Woman is an all-devouring curse...' He sighed and felt better. Hungry, he went to the kitchen, but retreated in the face of the unwashed pots and pans. Then, looking out in the direction that Tara and the children had gone, he felt a new inspiration: 'I go become a vegetarian.' He repeated this quietly to himself and, clapping his hands as his resolution grew, he repeated, 'I will, I will. A vegetarian's life na involve too much cooking. I go eat fruits an' boil vegetables.' He returned to his room to start another round of praying and meditating, beginning with deep-breathing exercises; but when he attempted a headstand, the blood rushed to his cheeks, his eyes bulged, and he felt both nauseated and terrified. Relaxing his hold, he wiped perspiration from his forehead and forlornly muttered, 'Ah, it hard indeed to be a swami.'

Chapter Two

At first Devan wasn't sure what was happening, as waves of memory kept coming back to him while he meditated. The sharpness of the images was frightening, but they were seductive too so that he indulged his fancy. He wasn't in the house anymore; he was with his mother – a mere child. Andar, the barber, grim-faced stood before him, large hands shifting his head in various positions; left, then right, his hair being snipped away. He hated having his hair cut, but his mother felt his hair was growing too quickly, and the neighbours would joke that he looked like a girl; once, laughing, they had even peeped between his legs to find out his real sex, all those baboon faces. Andar held him firmly as Devan fidgeted; he wanted to bite the barber's hands. 'Let him cut you hair, son,' urged Lachandai, his mother. But Devan suddenly couldn't stand it any longer, and jerked sideways. Just then Andar snipped, viciously. Devan winced. His mother moaned.

At once Devan saw blood leaking from between Andar's fingers, and felt a stinging pain in his left ear. It burned! More blood, and Devan let out such a howl that the entire village thought Andar was trying to murder him. His mother lamented, 'Oh Gawd, me son – Andar you want fo' kill he, man! Eh-eh!' She almost swooned, and Devan bawled even more as he watched the stupefied expression on Andar's face.

From then on Lachandai vowed never to take him to a barber again, and decided to cut his hair herself, which meant rarely, and Devan's hair grew very long: he even started looking like a girl, and one villager mockingly called him a *bramchari*, a wandering holy man with long hair. But Devan liked how the word sounded and he laughed. Next he looked at his hair in the mirror and saw how long it had become, and he laughed again.

When his mother came at him with a pair of scissors, Devan pretended he was going to be murdered again. 'Ow, son, you hair too long,' she cajoled him, 'you growing up, son, soon you go be a big man,' but Devan ran away from her and Lachandai doted on him so much she would never press the matter. His father, Chattergoon, wire-thin and dark, who had come from India as a boy and learned the value of hard work early in life, watched from a distance and said: 'Devan mus' learn a trade.' His sinewy frame shook a little as he watched his son; he knew Devan wasn't doing too well at school. His teachers said it was because of his ungovernable temper, but privately Chattergoon thought his son was hopeless, though he didn't confide this to his wife. Why did Mr. Kumar, his teacher, make Devan spend all his time gardening, that part of the curriculum reserved for dunces? He had begged Mr. Kumar to give Devan one last chance; but Mr. Kumar shook his head and Chattergoon knew that the boy's only hope lay in learning a trade.

Devan saw himself standing before Gosai, a bald and oily man with black protuberant lips, the owner of Gosai's Tailoring Establishment. He was reluctant to take Devan: something about the boy made him a little nervous. But Lachandai pleaded with him: 'Ow, you mus' take my son.'

'How old is he?'

'Fifteen now.'

Gosai continued looking at Devan, he still wasn't sure, and he chewed tobacco, thinking. Devan inhaled some of the foul smell of the tobacco and his heart beat faster. Then Gosai scratched his head, a gesture which Devan thought ominous.

'Arright, I goin' to mek him learn.'

The finality in Gosai's voice pleased Chattergoon and Lachandai, but caused the opposite reaction in Devan, a resentment which would return from time to time in urgent, spirited flashes.

On the first day Devan got his initiation as an apprentice

when Gosai hit him on his head with a pair of scissors. He vowed never to forget that blow. Never! He would bide his time. As part of his apprentice's lot he had to take care of Gosai's elaborate flower garden in front of his house; he had to cut the grass and pull out the weeds which grew plentifully. Devan even thought that the weeds grew spitefully and were in conspiracy with Gosai to make him work. When Gosai bought a filly Devan knew at once it would be he who had to take care of it. At first the filly kicked as Devan drew close, but then beast and boy eyed each other, and Devan smiled, and going closer, murmured to it: 'Ho, boy, ho.'

Gosai heard him and laughed, and Devan felt the laughter echo in his ears and right then he remembered the blow from the pair of scissors on the first day. Gosai walked away, and Devan watched the filly which came near to him, auspiciously he thought, and allowed him to curry it. He began slowly, enjoying the sensation now. 'Ho, girl, ho,' he cooed to it. 'I hate all o' dem. You's me only friend.'

Now only about half an hour each day was spent on learning how to cut and stitch. Devan, after cutting the grass, weeding and currying the horse for the ninth time that day thought about this, particularly when the other assistants came and watched him from the window. Devan decided to protest. He said to Gosai, 'You tink I could become a tailor by waterin' yuh flower garden, eh?'

Gosai stopped pedalling on his Singer sewing machine and looked at Devan in disbelief. He passed a hand slowly across his pate.

'An' cut grass? An' brush de haas?'

Gosai's assistants stopped pedalling, and one sniggered. Blood rushed to the tips of Devan's ears, and he stammered more of his protest, which caused the assistants to snigger even more. Gosai slowly got up and eyed Devan menacingly. 'So you na want to water me flower-garden eh?'

'No! I want to be a tailor!'

Gosai again passed his hand across his pate, leant back all of a sudden and burst out laughing uncontrollably. The assistants took this uncharacteristic action as a cue and they also laughed, loudly, and one pointed at Devan and sneered at him.

Devan, unable to bear this any longer and remembering the blow to his head on the first day, grabbed the nearest pair of scissors and hit out blindly. Gosai howled with pain, and blood dripped from his forehead. Devan became panic-stricken for a moment as he looked in disbelief at what he had done. Then realization came to him, and he bolted as fast as he could, still armed with the scissors. The assistants took after him through the streets of the village, but Devan ran like the devil was after him, outsprinting them and everyone else who followed, for in no time villagers came from every direction, all expressing horror at what Devan had done, some lamenting loudly at seeing Gosai's swollen head and the blood still dripping close to his right eye.

When he heard the news, Chattergoon lamented bitterly. 'Ow Bhagawan, wha' dis come pon me life now! Devan is a rascal!' Lachandai wept: she wept before Mrs. Gosai, and before Mr. Gosai's assistants, each time begging that her son be forgiven. She did this for an entire week, entreating everyone who cared to listen. Eventually a compromise was reached when Chattergoon agreed to weed Gosai's yard with its plentiful grass for an entire year without pay. And Lachandai promised to pay for all the articles which Gosai said Devan had stolen.

Now Devan stayed at home and did nothing which, for a while, he liked. Then he became bored, unhappy. He even refused to help on Chattergoon's small farm, his idleness irking his father, and before long Chattergoon started believing his son had really stolen Gosai's articles and he quietly, then loudly, started complaining about it and about Devan's laziness. Devan, unable to bear this any longer, one day responded hotly. At once his mother chided him for being rude. Devan made a loud clacking sound with his lips, teeth and tongue pulled together and apart in an instinctive act. And Chattergoon, incensed at this sucking of the teeth, cried out:

'You go have to leave dis house if you tink you go lie

aroun' an' do not'ing all day!' He was assailed by the memory of his own growing up after coming from India and the hard work everyone did then to survive in British Guiana; Devan was doomed if he didn't learn the value of hard work from early. But Devan sulked and kept to himself. Lachandai would go up to him and try to pamper him, telling him to obey his father, always. She cajoled softly. 'What you want fo' turn, Devan? A *bramchari*?' She smiled, because she knew Devan remembered the childhood image, and, playing up to her, he nodded. Lachandai laughed. Devan figured the word *bramchari* had something to do with holiness and reverence as well as loafing around; in a way he was pleased by it.

But Chattergoon, his old bones almost rattling, fumed and scolded and moved threateningly towards Devan, who resisted with folded fists. Lachandai burst into tears. 'Ow me Gawd, you is a big man now, eh? You want to fight wid yuh fader!' She wept even more. Devan couldn't stand this any longer and he rushed into his room and bolted the door. Now he felt the entire world was against him, he would stay in his room and starve himself to death. Yes, that would satisfy his parents! But after a while he began to like the sequestered calm of his room: it made him feel independent, and he laughed to himself even though he was beginning to feel hungry. Again he thought, bramchari, yes, he would remain the entire day without eating; he would develop self-control. He knew too that his parents would get worried about him if he didn't eat and a sense of power, of being able to manipulate them, came to him. And Lachandai, fearing that her son would die from starvation, began beating her breast and, speaking loudly so that Devan could hear her, blamed Chattergoon: 'Ow, man, na worry he. He is big boy now!'

Devan heard this and tried to resist tittering, for the longer he stayed in his room the more he felt able to control his hunger pangs, and he experienced a strange thrill the more his mother cried out loudly for him to hear. Lachandai added, 'Dat boy is not a child anymore, man. He full-eye now.' Chattergoon looked at her, then at the room where Devan had locked himself in and let out in a rasp:

'Is time we marry he!'

In the silence that followed Devan felt a jolt which was intense, all his former feelings of control disappearing.

Chattergoon added, 'A wife go teach him fo' be responsible!'

Devan burst out of his room at once. 'No! No! I don't want to get married!' He shouted this over and over again and threatened to go back to his room and bolt himself in for an entire week.

'Oh, no!' cried Lachandai, beating her frail breasts.

Chattergoon dourly repeated that a wife would teach him to become responsible, and they continued quarrelling like this for a long while. Devan, from time to time, would lock himself in once more and again feel the calm of being sequestered, but this didn't last too long because Lachandai would cook his favourite dish and entice him out of the room. 'Son,' she said, 'you full-eye now.'

But Devan still insisted that he didn't want to marry, he was only seventeen, while his father complained that he was lazy, ungrateful, and a thief, and Lachandai, in softer tones, said that if he married he'd receive the blessings of God. Devan looked at her, thinking, mulling this over, wishing he was back in his room, even though he wouldn't bolt the door this time. When Chattergoon repeated his charges, Devan in exasperation let out that he would marry – but he wouldn't marry someone he didn't see beforehand. A week later, however, Chattergoon had a surprise for him. With a wide smile on his face he said to Devan:

'Son, you lucky.'

'What for?' Devan was suspicious at once, knowing that his father was full of guile.

'De gal parents got cows.'

'Lots of them, Devan,' chimed his mother quickly.

'What I care for cows, eh?' Devan shot back, looking at his father as if he was about to fold his fists once more.

'What you care for, eh? Haas?' Chattergoon shouted.

For a second Devan thought about Gosai's filly. A smile crept across his face as he more clearly remembered the animal and how he used to curry it; and Chattergoon watching him was confused and shook his head. Lachandai muttered, 'We a' Hindu, son. Cow betta than haas.'

But Devan insisted on seeing the girl first before committing himself; he knew that once he set eyes on her he'd be displeased and that would be the end of the matter. But again Chattergoon harangued him for his ingratitude.

'Okay, I go marry she!' Devan blurted out resignedly. Chattergoon looked at Lachandai and smiled, while Devan grimaced. And for many nights after Devan kept grimacing and wondering what kind of girl his wife would be, what she would look like. Why wasn't he allowed to see her until the day of the wedding? Sequestered in his room, though the door was wide open, he thought about their Hindu traditions and muttered loudly, 'Stupid custom, stupid custom.' He repeated this over and over again, even while he ate; first to Lachandai, then to Chattergoon; but the latter laughed and said that a wife would teach him to be responsible.

On the day of the wedding, as the guests began arriving, Devan began feeling a strange thrill: he suddenly realised that he was the centre of all the attention, that he liked the fuss being made over him. His excitement mounted as he watched the large crowd, the men dressed in their white shirts and their hair greased with Brylcream and unscented vaseline; the women, especially the older ones, in their saris, everyone gleaming. Devan beamed happily at them. Then he saw someone in a saffron sari, glittering with gold jewellery and looking at him steadily; his heart thumped. Mrs. Gosai. His heart thumped even more as he looked around for the tailor, sinking with each face that looked vaguely familiar. When he didn't see Gosai, he felt better and began smiling again.

Two hours later, the *barriat*, with his relatives (many of whom he didn't know existed) and a number of other male guests, took off to the bride's home at Tarlogie on the Corentyne, all in hired taxis. It was a real excursion; everyone wanted to have a happy time, and Devan's marriage provided the occasion. On the longish, winding road, the *barriat* passed village after village, the occasional cow or donkey straggling across and causing the taxis to veer suddenly left, then right. And men, women and children alongside the Corentyne road waved from the artesian wells – mostly Indians, and only a few Africans – and the relatives leaned out of the taxis and joyfully waved back, some slapping the sides and doors as they screamed out their greetings – the atmosphere one of a fast-paced carnival.

Watching all this, Devan felt even more exhilarated. The Corentyne wind blowing from across the Atlantic Ocean bordering the Guianese coast tingled his nostrils with the pungency of crabgrass and shrimp. For the moment he gave no thought to what his wife would look like. Only the din filled his ears, the hands waving at him, some raising handkerchiefs. He caught a glimpse of his father, how grave he looked one moment, happy the next, as one taxi raced another, and Devan regretted just then that he hadn't decided to get married earlier, and he too leaned out of the window and slapped the sides of the Toyota to add to the din and revelry.

At Tarlogie, another crowd was there ready to greet them, and Devan nodded to everyone and smiled continually despite the sun's heat and the overcrowding from too many guests and the oppressive smell of *puri* in the air. Someone came forward, tall, saintly-looking, the pandit smelling of ghee. He greeted Devan and said he was eager to get on with the ceremony. The pandit was so authoritative in his demeanour that Devan couldn't help but keep his eyes on him, despite all the excitement around as more beaming faces peered at him. Where was the bride? The pandit once more glanced at him, and Devan decided he would have to be patient; he was ready for the ceremony to begin.

Devan saw her, veiled, head lowered; she seemed so shy. The pandit began preaching on the sanctity of marriage under the bamboo and zinc tent, about the need to live spiritual lives according to the laws of Krishna. Devan watched some of the elders nod sentimentally, as if they were the ones getting married all over again, and he too nodded as the tall pandit watched him gravely. Then he turned, eager to catch a glimpse of his bride behind the veil, eager to see her face. What would she look like? Some of the guests, the young ones, tittered, and the pandit immediately raised his voice in command. Devan couldn't help being impressed at how he controlled his audience, how everyone looked up to him as he spoke, the power he exerted. And the words flowed, everyone listening with rapt attention, including his father. For a while Devan forgot that he was the one getting married, and he listened carefully to each word the pandit uttered, at his manner of articulation, and how the audience continued to nod, to express approval constantly. Now the pandit was quoting freely from the Hindu holy texts; Devan was mesmerised, and he muttered to himself, 'I go be a man of God; I go have a mission in life.' He repeated this once more, his imagination now taking him beyond the Tarlogie pandit, so clear the vision was. And before he knew it, the ceremony was over and the gifts started pouring in, and this too was a surprise.

His mood changed, and with arms wide open he received the plentiful china and dollar notes pressed into his palm, and he muttered now, 'I go be a rich man too-beside.' He laughed to himself, his eyes brightening. Then he closed his eyes and a soft prayer involuntarily broke from his lips. It was then that his bride lifted her head from its lowered position. Sensing her movement Devan opened his eyes and saw her. She was dark-skinned! All along he was hoping that she'd be fair. 'God curse me,' he lamented in a low tone.

Puzzled by this reaction, his wife once more lowered her head. Devan looked around for the pandit, his thoughts in mild disarray. Had he left, he wondered. Dismay grew on him, but as more gifts started pouring in, his gloom lifted. He was still struck by images of the pandit pontificating to the wedding-guests; and he imagined himself doing this, controlling the audience. He smiled. Everyone looked at him and laughed, because they thought he was really very pleased with his bride. Even Chattergoon laughed now. In Devan's mind, everything was happening so fast.

On the way back to Providence Village he laughed again to himself, thinking about the pandit and the numerous gifts he'd received. The driver of the taxi laughed companionably. Devan was still laughing to himself when they arrived back in Providence, and Chattergoon, shaking his head, wondered about his son. And even at that solemn moment when Lachandai went forward to greet Tara, and she, as was the custom, lowered her head to Lachandai's feet, Devan was still smiling to himself.

For months after, as if he was in a spell, Devan kept thinking about the Tarlogie pandit. Now Tara began to wonder about him; eyeing him suspiciously from time to time. Things came to a head one evening when Devan announced that he would begin meditating: 'I go be a man of destiny; a great man too.'

'A what?' Tara asked, not sure she heard correctly.

'A man of God.'

'Oh?'

'Yes-yes.' His eyes gleamed, and Tara smiled dutifully, though doubtfully. For a while she didn't take him seriously; maybe it was just a whim. But when he started locking himself in his room day after day and gathering a pile of Hindu books, she knew he was serious. When her patience wore thin the questioning began.

She said, 'Why you not say on yuh wedding day dat you go stay home an' meditate all de time, eh?' And Devan, in reply would ask: 'What about de cows you father promise?'

'Cows, eh?' she scoffed. 'You want cows, eh?' And she laughed mockingly.

Lachandai visited them from time to time and listened to them argue and she would go home and report to Chattergoon, who no longer responded. When Lachandai visited again she brought food, and she handed Tara a few dollar bills. A year passed quickly and Jotish was born, and Devan decided to stop meditating for a while. He assisted in Chattergoon's farm and then attempted barbering, then tailoring, but nothing really pleased him. Shanti and Devi were born quickly after, and Lachandai became an even more frequent visitor. Devan spent more time in Chattergoon's rice field, but one day, his back aching from bending over in the paddy swamp, the image of the Tarlogie pandit returned.

That evening he once more locked himself in his room and meditated; he wouldn't go to the rice fields again but stay at home and dwell on God, always. He knew his life's work, his destiny.

Tara had been at her wit's end to make him stop his meditating. She even tried hiding his books. By now Devan was convinced she was working for the Devil as he told his mother, then his father, who groaned unhappily. It was from then that Tara really threatened to leave him.

And now, after she had really left, Devan went to the window to look for her only out of habit, knowing indeed that she wouldn't come back. As he stood there and recalled his son's face he sighed a little; Tara's face came back to him too and, once in a while, the faces of his daughters.

But at the back of his mind was the thought that it was his destiny to be alone and think upon God – this only. Nothing else, no one else, mattered.

Chapter Three

'I mus' live a life of discipline,' he repeated to himself, slowly, then in a chanting manner, and the words echoed in his mind as if they were entering a deep tunnel, then they assumed the dimension of a full-length hymn until he wasn't sure what he was saying. But sometimes his mind was filled with palpable images: his son gathering hibiscus flowers and Gosai's filly rearing up before him like a full-grown horse and snorting. Getting up he hurried to the window, hoping he might see Tara coming down the road. Instead he saw Lachandai, an aluminium saucepan in her hand, the basket barely concealing it, and he realised right then that he was hungry.

'She na go come back, son. You mus' stop looking out,' Lachandai told him when she got inside.

But he was busy eating the curried channa and rice, real vegetarian that he now was. Lachandai smiled at him dotingly, 'You mus' pray, Devan, dat she never go come back.' He stopped eating and looked at her sternly and muttered, 'Eh?' and immediately thought of the familiar phrase, 'Woman is an all-devouring evil.' He was about to say it out loud to his mother when she looked away.

'People a talk, son,' Lachandai continued. 'Maybe it good Tara lef'.'

Talk? Yes, he'd heard some of it himself, but only about his zeal for devotion, though some had questioned that he could be a man of God and yet be married, the incongruity of holiness and carnality. He had resolved this in his mind – and besides, Tara had left. It was his destiny now to live a life of celibacy and abstinence. He stopped eating, and Lachandai, watching him, muttered that some of the older villagers had recalled him banging Gosai on his head: to them it didn't seem like such a long time ago. She smiled but Devan pointedly ignored her. Lachandai, thinking her son wanted to be left alone to meditate, quietly left him to walk back to be with Chattergoon, defiant against everyone and steadfast in her belief in her son's destiny. *Let them talk*. But when one had dared say, 'Maybe Tara had to put up with much. No wonda she lef',' they were assailed by Lachandai's strident voice: 'She too lazy, she refuse to obey she husband. No wonda Devan ask she to leave!'

Chattergoon watched his wife's performance in studied fascination. Was it true that Devan was walking the streets alone, affecting a sanctimonious expression all the time, heavy volumes under his arm? Chattergoon wondered, still looking at Lachandai. She talked about Devan's destiny and his devotion to their Hindu religion. He thought about India, that place he dreamt about so often, the long journey as a boy on the ship, the rat holes, the indentured labour after. He felt it in his bones. That too was a destiny that had to be fulfilled. Was this Devan's? Everything was predetermined. Lachandai was still muttering about her son and about what people were saying. Chattergoon decided to keep his thoughts to himself.

In the meantime, Devan had taken to sitting in villagers' neatly cow-dung plastered bottom-houses, and talking to two, three, then four villagers about Hinduism. He found receptive ears and, as word got around, more came. Devan, remembering the Tarlogie pandit, affected the guise of the scholar, he pontificated, he quoted from the *Vedas*; his audience was impressed. They leant forward, they wanted to hear more; he played upon their deepest yearnings, the same as his father's, the same talk about India, the nostalgia and surprising forlornness. He regaled them with all that he read, feeding their longing to know that Hinduism was still integral to their lives and was now finding an expression in serious discussion outside the Hindu temple, which only a few attended anyway. His talk began to have the zeal, people said, of the Christian's, they in their churches and meeting halls. Yes, Devan was a preacher, the older ones felt, forgetting entirely the incident with Gosai.

And Devan grew bolder in his discussions of the Hindu scriptures, as he talked about the soul and the necessity for it to be free from its corporeal prison, the phrases rolling off his tongue, delighting him as much as they overwhelmed his audience. And some begged, 'Explain, Devan... Swami.'

'Ah, de vile body – you see,' he replied, solemnly, and he pounded his chest and declaimed once more against the vile body. He looked at their faces, the awe. And not unexpectedly, word got round, from bottom-house to bottom-house, and before long Devan found himself covering entire streets and, on Sundays, when no one worked, they came, a dozen at a time, to listen to him. He invited questions from his audience, pretending now to be a sort of seer. Soon, though, he tried a different tactic. He would ask the questions first in case they asked him something he didn't know about. In particular, he feared the youths at the fringe of his audience: they were rascals, he could tell from their eyes, they treated him merely as a curiosity. He would confound them, and he adopted the manner of the schoolmaster.

'Who's de greatest poet?' he began in a show of high-spiritedness.

'Shakespeare,' came the quick reply.

Everyone listened attentively, they liked this disputation, with Devan clad in white, his hair growing longer – the bramchari as he was. He smiled at his audience. 'Wrong,' he replied.

'Milton.'

'Wrong-wrong.'

'Rabindranath Tagore,' insisted another youth. 'He write the *Gitanjili*; he won the Nobel prize an' he born in India.'

Devan laughed in the face of the questioner. 'Still wrong,' he said smugly.

'Who then? Tell we!' they insisted.

'Kalidas,' he replied, with a huge grin.

None of them had heard of Kalidas and the older ones, as Devan expected, murmured approval. He quickly rattled off a few lines from Kalidas, and the older ones insisted that Devan was correct and chided the youngsters for showing poor manners, they should have more respect for one so learned. But they giggled, to Devan's dismay.

When Devan returned home, his thoughts still on the youngsters, he rifled through the pages of his books and realised that he'd been quoting from Rudyard Kipling instead of Kalidas. At first he was embarrassed, but then it struck him how easy it was to fool everyone. 'Kipling indeed,' he muttered, and once more a vision of the Tarlogie pandit crossed his mind. Then, more soberly, he wondered if the latter's quotations were sometimes also incorrect, but of course no one would know the difference.

The more he dwelled on this, the less it seemed necessary to study his heavy volumes so rigorously; it was work that was demanding too much concentration. Perhaps his other habits, his resolve to live ascetically, were also unnecessary, and there was no need for him to deny himself his favourite fare any longer; no need to fast for a whole day and try to develop willpower by withstanding the needs of the stomach in the struggle of mind and spirit over body. Wasting no more time he grabbed a handful of bananas and ate quickly to his heart's content. His stomach primed, he yawned, then got up and went to the window, and looked down the main road once again. Thoughts of Jotish weighed heavily on his mind and he wondered if his son would turn into a rascal like the village youths. The thought made him angry and he only calmed himself down by recalling images of Jotish gathering the large-petalled hibiscus flowers from the neighbours' hedges for the *puja* he performed, and of Jotish sitting with him with legs folded before a framed picture of the Hindu deities and humming the mantras with him. He was sad that Jotish was no longer around, and he blamed this squarely on Tara.

At that moment, Lachandai knocked on his door, opened

it and came in. In the saucepan was thickly curried chicken, the smell at once causing Devan to crinkle his nostrils; it was his favourite fare. He smiled, hesitated for a moment. Lachandai encouraged, 'Ah, son, you look so thin, na? So skinny you deh. You mus' eat.' Devan wasted no more time and plunged into the food; but looking at Lachandai, his mouth half-primed with the meat, his sense of commitment to vegetarianism coming back to him, he wondered if the Devil was getting the better of him. He swallowed a little, still thinking, not sure. But then, turning away from his mother, Devan hissed out at the Devil, 'Get out, get out!'

Lachandai wasn't sure what was the matter with him, not sure if she heard correctly, but she left all the same, a puzzled expression on her face. Later, at home, she told Chattergoon about this; the latter, increasingly taciturn and laconic, merely muttered: 'Maybe it's his mission.' Lachandai began to feel she didn't understand her husband now either.

That same night, before falling asleep, Chattergoon thought a great deal about the Hindu saints, the deities, what they signified. Each one had a particular purpose, a mission, he figured. Looking up at the ceiling, he concentrated harder; each saint's purpose was to promote goodness and truth in the world. Was this Devan's task in life too? His son a saint? He thought about India again, how far away their real homeland was, how they had been brought here on the South American coast. What for? Was that also really destiny? And Devan? He would keep a more careful eye on his son.

But the village youths were not impressed; Devan's preaching in the bottom-houses wove no spell on them. Devan was an eccentric, that was all, and they laughed mockingly at the idea expressed by some of the older, die-hard Hindus, that he might become a Hindu saint. Times had changed; they were in British Guiana, not India!

They planned to eavesdrop on Devan in his house, for they heard that he often practised his speech-making alone, sometimes even while doing a headstand, one tittered. Before long, three or four of them were climbing close to his window and peeping at his antics. When they saw him gesticulating, talking to himself, they jeered and made faces at the window. Devan saw them.

'Get away, you moderass rascils! Get away!' he shouted loudly from the window, shaking his fist, convinced that they were indeed agents of the Devil out to torment him: 'Devil's pickney you are! All o' you!'

An hour later, poised in a headstand, Devan was startled by a loud clattering. At first he thought it was rain, the heavy drops falling on the zinc roof, but when he looked out, he saw it was the boys again, pelting his house with bricks. His face suffused with blood, his ears red hot, he was about to curse them again when he checked himself and lamented: 'Is me destiny to hear their insults.' He vented his frustration by loudly sucking his teeth, the saliva against his lips and teeth making a sound like paper tearing. 'Illiterate beasts,' he cried softly, as he went back to his room to resume his meditation. Eyes closed tightly, he wished now he was far away from Providence village; he'd outgrown it; some place else was calling him, something else, even though he wasn't sure what. Vacantly he thought he heard the clatter of bricks again; this time though it was really rain.

Four

Devan had taken to reading about phrenology, an area of knowledge which intrigued him immensely. Since it often struck a chord with his own assessment of people, he saw in it a systematic base for his conclusions. But looking at his visitor, Pandit Gocolram from Mahaica, he was, though, at first confused. He focused on the pandit's low forehead and concluded that no doubt he wasn't gifted with much intellect, but the pandit's suave manner and beguiling laugh made him somewhat uneasy. He continued looking at Gocolram, at the angle the hair receded from the forehead, then the genial manner, and still he wasn't sure. Gocolram said, 'You see, Swami, I hear much 'bout you. I am really happy to meet you.' When Devan took the hand Gocolram extended, he noted how soft his fingers were, like the tendrils of a plant.

'I am delighted by you' visit, Pandit.'

'I been hear 'bout you as far as Mahaica,' offered Gocolram, looking away a little.

'Oh.' Devan beamed, no longer concentrating on the pandit's hands or forehead; he was flattered to hear that he was known as far as the East Coast of Demerara, his fame had indeed spread. And when Gocolram asked Devan to tell him more about himself, the latter did so eagerly, mentioning among other things the research project that was on his mind.

'It about Hindus in dis part of de world. The New World, you know, Panditji. We been cut off from we roots when white people bring we from India.'

This was a hackneyed subject to Gocolram, but he encouraged Devan to continue by nodding frequently, and the latter tittered a few times because at last he'd found a patient listener, and beamed as he talked about his life, his enthusiasm growing. Next he brought out his Hindu texts, mildewed and frayed, to show Gocolram, whose interest was perceptibly less than keen. Devan looked at the low forehead and this time he saw a slight grimace forming. He was alarmed. But Gocolram smiled again beguilingly, as he added:

'You mus' try to become a member of de All India League, Swamiji.'

Devan thought he hadn't heard correctly, his heart beat faster now, but recovering he cried: 'Yes-yes, I must!' He'd long cherished this idea, though it seemed an impossibility. From his father Devan had heard a great deal about the League, what an august organisation it was, and many times he'd seen it referred to in the newspapers with pictures of prominent League members shown donating money or cutting a ribbon to mark an important Hindu event. But all this was taking place in the capital city; Providence Village seemed so far removed from everything, he complained, but Gocolram at once assured him that the League wasn't really that aloof, wasn't out of reach for one like himself, though its members included some of the richest Hindus in Guiana, many being doctors and lawyers. Devan mumbled to himself in some confusion. Gocolram added with a genial smile:

'You see, Swami, you mus' let dem know wha' you do here, how devoted you is to our beloved religion.'

'Devoted, eh?' asked Devan, as if sceptical, thinking. Gocolram rattled on, 'Then somebody in the League's executive go sponsor you, dat's how.' Devan's face fell. Who would sponsor him? And Gocolram at once sensed his thoughts and drew closer to him, and in a brotherly way added: 'You mustn't worry, Swami. After all it tek a long time for me to become a member myself.'

'You? A member?' Devan blurted out, then not wanting to be disrespectful, started acknowledging the membership as if it were a well-known fact; a truism, which the whole world knew, and he tried smiling, unconsciously imitating Gocolram's beguiling manner. But the latter only laughed and began spelling out the number of charitable works the League had done over the years; Devan kept nodding all the while until he could feel his neck hurting; he also looked at Gocolram's forehead in a new light and it didn't seem low anymore, but even. And he kept being amazed that the man standing before him, in his own house, was a member of the august All India League; and, maybe, he too would become a member. He figured that Gocolram's visit was indeed the hand of destiny at work.

In continuing affability Gocolram added, 'You's someone really devoted to our great religion, far away as we are from India; or else our Hindu brothers and sisters na talk about you so much.'

'So much, eh?' Devan continued to be amazed.

'You see, before long you go become a member of the All India League and you'll be better known, even in Georgetown, you understand?'

Devan nodded approvingly, but what Gocolram said next made his heart sink. 'Ah, Swami, is a pity dem young people give yuh such a haad time. Dem prappa mannish.' Gocolram cleared his throat noisily as he said this, and self-pity welled up in Devan as he looked at Gocolram. So that too had spread around, the rascals! 'Dem prappa mannish,' Gocolram repeated slowly, carefully observing Devan's reactions.

'Yes, dem raskil!' Devan blurted out in agitation as he saw his dreams of becoming a member of the League disappear. Gocolram stepped back a few inches, amazed at this change of mood, but still managing a perfunctory smile. Devan looked at the man before him with some scepticism, unable to decide why he had mentioned the youngsters. But what Gocolram said next surprised him. 'You mus' come and live wid me in Mahaica, Swami. There the young people na bodder you. Maybe you can help me wid pandit work.' He smiled again. 'Our Hindu people dem gon be glad to hear you speak.'

Devan frowned, knitted his eyebrows in disbelief at this offer, not sure what he should say next, the hesitation causing

Gocolram to add, 'Na forget dat Mahaica is three times bigga than Providence, Swami.'

Devan's thoughts raced wildly, new aspirations and expectations flooding into his mind, overwhelming him, and he began thinking that he'd be closer to Georgetown, to the members of the All India League, the rich and influential – it was where he wanted to be! 'I will come, I will come!' he sang.

'To Mahaica, eh?' asked Gocolram, to be sure, inwardly pleased with himself, though for a moment, as he watched Devan almost squirming with pleasure at the offer, not poised like a swami anymore, he wondered if he'd done the right thing. But when he thought of the relief Devan would provide in taking on some of his pandit's chores, he dismissed the doubt from his mind and, shaking Devan's hand once more, he left.

The only way he could contain his excitement, Devan felt, was by meditating. And, folding his legs beneath him, he thanked God, thanked the hand of destiny at work, smiling all the while, his eyes closed, new expectations like light bulbs switching on and off in his brain. And the biggest bulb in his mind, giving out the brightest light, was the All India League. Then he started chanting as the lights kept flickering in his head, and he did this for the next two hours, all the while thanking God. He would be able to get rid of the village youths forever; but fleetingly he also thought of Jotish, of Tara; and then of Gocolram and the All India League.

A week later, suitcase in hand, he was ready to leave Providence village. Lachandai wept and said, 'Ow, son, God go be wid you. You mus' go.' Devan wasn't sure what he should say to her, or to his father who watched him closely, taciturn as ever, still not sure what to make of his son. Chattergoon thought merely of the bare house which he'd built with his own hands, what a useless effort it now seemed. Somehow Devan didn't seem like his own son anymore, with his hair long, his face thin; secretly he searched for a pious spark in his eyes, hoping he would see something that would really astonish him. When he didn't, his thoughts went back to India, as happened more and more as he got older. It was only when his wife spoke that those images flitted out of his mind and he found himself listening to her as she said to Devan:

'Ow, son, you mus' rememba Providence. Is hay yuh baan, where you ma an' pa live, where yuh chil'ren also baan, Jotish in particular, eh? Always rememba!'

FIVE

Mrs. Gocolram was a tallish, heavy-set woman with a wide mouth, indicative of brashness, thought Devan; she seemed distinctly opposite to her husband who was quietly-spoken and given to self-indulgent reflection in preference to action, as Devan quickly found out. Gocolram indeed spent much time in the polished upper flat of his house which everyone knew as the 'sanctum' and where the pandit's six children rarely ever visited.

Gocolram was convivial with Devan, though he would have wished to appear urbane, and even aloof, but this wasn't an integral part of his character – try as he did to show it from time to time – the result being that the two men got along really well and Devan began to feel equal to him, though never forgetting that Gocolram was a member of the All India League, a considerable step above him. Mrs.Gocolram was less welcoming; Devan felt she regarded him as a new but unpaying boarder, and her six children, always huddled about her, often looked at him as if they were ready to claw him at any moment.

It was on the first Sunday after he arrived that Gocolram said to him, 'Let's go to the Hindu temple, Swamiji.' He was grinning, eager to show off his protegé, whose impending visit he'd announced as an event that the Mahaica worshippers should welcome; saying generous things about Swami Devan, which, if the latter had known, would have deeply overwhelmed, not to say immensely flattered him. Of course, Gocolram was hoping that a warm welcome from the Mahaica Hindus would make Devan want to stay permanently; he could train him in due course to assist with his pandit's duties. If he played his cards correctly he might even succeed in making Devan a member of the League, and then Devan would be eternally grateful to him.

The large crowd at the temple made Devan's head spin, and he thanked God at once and wished Tara was present to see him. There were no Providence rascals here, only the faces of staunch Hindus before him and his heart warmed towards them, even though he was anxious. The perceptive Gocolram muttered, 'Be confident, Swami. You're greatly admired here.' Devan attempted a smile to indicate that all was well. The air reeked of incense, sweet-smelling dyes, and an assortment of perfumes. Everything seemed auspicious.

It was time for him to speak, and Devan got up and called everyone brothers and sisters and, with an ease which surprised him, thinking of himself as the Tarlogie pandit, he waxed warm, as they to him, and, growing more confident in a tremulous sort of way, his short arms jutting out, he exhorted everyone to cherish the principles of Hinduism since it was the world's first religion. He encouraged them to read the Hindu scriptures frequently, daily, if possible; to teach their young Hinduism, to meditate as often as possible and to shun the materialistic way. 'Purity of body and soul,' he called out in a tone of rising fervour, 'Yes, dat's what you should aim at, eh? The soul mus' dwell in everyday harmony with the Creator of the Universe. Den God go know you, 'cause we're all One Big Soul, na? We are together, in the big and wide universe. *Acha!*' After another hour of this, all the while gesticulating and changing the tone of his voice as he recalled the Tarlogie pandit doing, he bowed and, clasping his hands in the satisfied manner of a man who believed he'd done a good job and now awaited the adulation due him, he took his seat. Loud applause followed, and Gocolram whispered to him, 'Splendid orat'ry, Swami. You spoke well.'

Devan, still glowing with the heat of his delivery, with the applause ringing in his ears, smiled and bowed steadily to his audience. Right then he figured he'd made the right decision to come to Mahaica; now, indeed, Providence Village was far from his mind.

After the service some of the older Hindus, given to doting flattery, came and shook his hand and told him what a fine speech he gave and, as was the custom, presented him with gifts of rice, bananas, squash, and sometimes money. Devan held the dollar notes tightly and smiled again, exhorting them earnestly to live a life of piety. When everyone was gone he gathered all his fruits and provisions into a sack and hugging it closely to him like a prized possession, he looked at Gocolram. The latter, also smiling, asked, 'Would you preach again next Sunday, Swamiji?'

'Of course,' Devan replied, fingers still clutching his sack, and he imagined the temple packed with people, all coming to hear him, the word spreading everywhere. Gocolram looked at him curiously.

Later that evening in his sanctum, the crickets whirring outside in the Mahaica night air, Gocolram, stirring from a moment of contemplation, said to him, 'You win their hearts, Swamiji. Ah, me very pleased wid you performance.' He watched Devan smiling happily, like a child almost, and for a moment he wondered if he'd made a mistake in bringing him to Mahaica. But he dismissed this thought from his mind and forced himself to dwell on some of the swami's words, said earlier at the temple, especially about holiness and truth.

The next day, and the day after, Devan counted his fruits and vegetables. He did this again after his next visit to the temple, the crowds giving him more gifts, which Gocolram felt he even encouraged a little in the emphasis on the blessedness of giving in his address. On each visit, more gifts poured in and Devan watched his sacks grow larger and, occasionally, before retiring for the night, he pulled them out from under the bed and inspected them. For a time Gocolram humoured Devan's pleasure in accumulation, but one night he said to his wife, 'You mus' mek use of some of Swami provision.'

Mrs. Gocolram heaved in her agreement.

It was when Devan returned from a speaking engagement outside Mahaica, Hindus now inviting him everywhere to speak, that adding some gifts to his stock, he noticed that it had dwindled. He cried out, 'Thieves!' At once he suspected Mrs. Gocolram, but he waited until the pandit left the house before he marched down to the lower flat and accused her of the theft.

'What kinda charge is dis you bring 'pon Gocolram household, eh?' Mrs. Gocolram shrieked intimidatingly, and Devan, his heart sinking, then said it must have been the children who'd stolen his bananas – he remembered his own love for bananas as a child. But Mrs Gocolram, all fired up, her large breasts shaking against the thin beige cotton dress with spangled flowers, raged on: 'Pandit go hear 'bout dis! He bound to!' She always referred to her husband as 'pandit,' even in bouts of love-making. 'He must! He must!' Devan's heart sank deeper, for he suddenly realised how ungracious he might sound to Gocolram and he wished he'd never raised the theft at all.

He tried to pacify her, but to no avail. The truculent children, now around her, eyed him malevolently and Devan imagined them all on top of him, pushing him down, smashing him to a pulp, and Mrs. Gocolram right on top of the heap pressing her weight down, with her lips pursed in steely determination.

'You always accuse me children of mekking too much noise! I hear you tell pandit dat every day. I know, I know!' she crowed vehemently, her breath swirling round Devan like a pall of strange sickness, and he retreated, rushing out of the door as if chased by a swarm of killer bees.

Outside, feeling forlorn, he sat under a large mango tree a few yards from the house and listened to the leaves rustling until his spirit felt calmer, but glancing up every so often in case Mrs. Gocolram should come out after him. After a while he closed his eyes and meditated; it was the only way to ward off the evil she had cast. When he opened his eyes he saw two chestnut horses prancing, one on top of the other. He watched them closely, forgetting all about Mrs. Gocolram now. 'Beautiful animals,' he muttered unselfconsciously, and he remembered how fond he had been of Gosai's filly. The more he watched the horses, the more absorbed and relaxed he became and he was so obsessed with the horses' rhythmic movements that he didn't notice Gocolram walking up to him.

'Ah, you watchin' nature at work, Swami,' said the pandit, smiling.

Devan was startled and speechless with embarrassment, the blood rushing to the tips of his ears.

'Nothing to be ashamed of, Swami. Rememba Shiva an' Parvati. Haas not different from elephants you know.' Gocolram said affably.

'Yes-yes,' muttered a quickly agreeing Devan, thinking of the legend alluded to, but more concerned now about what Mrs. Gocolram had told her husband. But Gocolram put him at ease by saying, 'I have good news, you know.'

'You do?'

'Yes. An important visitor coming to Mahaica tomorrow.'

'Important? Who?'

'An executive of the All India League.'

Devan's heart beat faster, and Gocolram smiled beguilingly. 'Yes. Mr. Bhairam Bhuraji; he'll be here in person.'

The incident with Mrs. Gocolram was now completely gone from his mind; he wanted to know exactly what time, what they must do to make this important visitor's stay pleasant, happy. He tittered with excitement, and Gocolram watched him curiously, with a dim smile. Devan continued to reflect on the name of one whom he'd read about frequently in the newspapers, who was perhaps the biggest philanthropist in British Guiana. Such a man was worth knowing. Gocolram said, 'Mr. Bhairam do more for Hinduism than anyone else in dis country. Christian and Muslim respect him too.'

Devan nodded, thoughts in a flurry. 'You say he come tomorrow, eh?' His tone was ingratiating, as if he didn't really believe he would get to meet Mr. Bhairam, and Gocolram chuckled and kept reassuring him that Mr. Bhairam was indeed coming, pleased at the effect his words were having on Devan, and he added: 'You know, Swami, he come to Mahaica many times. He was responsible fo' building the Hindu temple.'

'Yes, indeed,' said Devan, too delighted to say much else.

'He come to meet the members of our blessed temple. I go arrange fo' you to meet him.'

Devan had assumed that this would be so, and he looked oddly at the other. Gocolram smiled his usual smile, but Devan was too excited to be fazed; he was convinced that the hand of destiny was really at work. What Gocolram said next seemed, in a strange way, to confirm this feeling, though it also confused and puzzled him.

'Mr Bhairam has the best race haas in Guiana.'

Devan instinctively looked around for the pair of chestnut horses, now beyond a cluster of trees not too far from the house. But as he looked, his eyes caught the windows of the house itself where he thought he saw someone. Mrs Gocolram? And as he recalled her large mouth, loud voice and railing manner, he grimaced.

'Haas, eh?' he eventually answered in reply to Gocolram, the grimace still etched on his face.

'Don't you like haas, Swami?'

'Oh, yes. I train one before, you know.' He was thinking of Gosai's filly again, and a smile replaced the grimace. Gocolram nodded sagely.

'Ah, me gon' tell Mr. Bhairam dat. He'll be pleased wid you, Swami.'

Devan looked at Gocolram and wasn't sure what to say next. He glanced around once more for the pair of chestnut horses, and Gocolram followed his eyes, but neither could see the animals now, as if their fleeting presence had been a miracle. Reflecting on this, Devan wondered if it was a good omen for the impending visit of the executive member of the All India League. Gocolram led the way back to the house, and Devan, unable to resolve this in his mind, was seized by a strange feeling of forlornness.

SIX

The scent of freshly-cut jasmines filled the air, and Devan breathed in heavily as he concentrated on God, the Supreme Consciousness, the Giver of all Life; he concentrated harder than ever, and Gocolram did the same. Then, together, in the upper flat, the sanctum, they prayed loudly, chanting next in unison, though Gocolram more to accord with Devan. After an hour of this, Gocolram stretched out his legs, for he was unable to keep them folded much longer in such an unbearable position as the lotus. He glanced at Devan from time to time, detecting a greater zeal for piety in him than ever. Was it all because of Mr. Bhairam's expected arrival? Closing his eyes again, he heard his guest breathe in heavily, making a sound like a wheeze one moment, a clear, soft inhalation the next, then air was let out with in a similar pattern, the rhythm almost lulling Gocolram who was wondering what thoughts were really going through Devan's breast. On impulse, with eyes still closed, he muttered to Devan: 'He go be here soon, Swami. Mr. Bhairam never fail to turn up.' No reply came, only the sound of wheezing which indicated a deep-chested inhalation, and then the air was let out quickly after. Gocolram found to his surprise that Devan's eyes were still closed, so he added, 'He generous too, fond of giving gifts.' Devan's eyes opened just then, even though he didn't really look alert, and he asked almost absent-mindedly, 'Gifts eh?'

They heard the sound of a car outside and at once they got up and sprinted down the stairs to see Mr. Bhairam's Mercedes parked outside; Gocolram a little in front, as always, and Devan, looking at his watch, very impressed that Mr. Bhairam came exactly when he said he would. 'Welcome,

welcome,' Gocolram cried in a spirited voice Devan hadn't heard before; Devan hung behind expectantly. Mr. Bhairam was tall, his paunch and benign expression giving him a friendly air, and Devan smiled continually as he waited to be introduced. He took in Mr. Bhairam's well-tailored blue suit, inhaled Old Spice cologne and studied the hair neatly combed backwards with Mohini Hair Oil. Mr. Bhairam's nails were neatly manicured as well, and when he pressed his lapels and showed his extremely white teeth – though one tooth on the left side of his mouth was gold-capped – he looked distinguished, unlike the Hindus Devan was used to seeing.

Gocolram was taking an everlastingly long time to introduce Devan; when he did, Devan became aware of Mr. Bhairam's habit of frowning, his thick eyebrows threatening to converge on his somewhat fleshy nose, a mannerism which really baffled Devan.

'So you're Swami Devan,' said Bhairam.

'Yes, indeed,' replied Devan, a little sheepishly, looking at the heavy eyebrows whose mobility suggested their seeming independence from the rest of the face.

'Do you know the *Gita* well? As well as Pandit Gocolram says you do?' asked the voice of authority, though not haughtily, for Mr. Bhairam seemed incapable of such a trait.

'Is me favourite book.'

And Gocolram, not to be left out, added: 'Swami reads night an' day, an' meditates too.'

Mr Bhairam frowned again, though this time Devan was not quite so surprised. Gocolram continued: 'He been speaking as far as Beterverwagting.'

Mr. Bhairam looked at Devan's short stature and smiled benignly, at which point Devan let out, like a muffled cry: 'I want to be a member of the All India League!'

Mr. Bhairam was taken aback at this sudden expression and this time his frown was matched by a penetrating look at Devan – who was on the point of apologising for his rashness – and said, somewhat gravely, 'First you have to prove yourself. Our organisation–'

But Gocolram intervened once more. 'Swami fasts often, an' he a good vegetarian.'

Bhairam, again looking at Devan's short stature, wondered what else he did. Devan, meantime, was thinking how much he owed Gocolram; but when the pandit started mentioning Devan's humble origins, how his father Gautum Lall Chattergoon was a small rice farmer in Providence Village far away in the county of Berbice, Devan's heart sank; his eyes closed automatically in despair, convinced now that his hopes were really dashed, for he knew how rich the Hindus in Georgetown were, and even some on the East Coast of Demerara; no, he would never be able to become a member of the All India League.

But Mr. Bhairam's response was surprising. 'Swami, you should have told me your father is Gautum Lall Chattergoon; I've heard about him from my own father, you see. The two of them came on the same ship from India, such a long time ago. They were both young boys then, my father being fourteen at the time and yours, maybe seven or eight. Is your *bhap* still living?' A bright smile flashed across the executive's face as he looked at Devan warmly now. And for the first time Devan saw his father as a man of some importance, and guiltily recalled the incidents in the past that kept them apart, how over the last three years he'd hardly spoken to his father, and he wished now he could make things up with him. Looking steadily at Mr. Bhairam, Devan said he was interested in doing research on the first East Indians who came to Guiana, something he'd been thinking about for a long time, since he was a boy in fact. This too pleased Mr. Bhairam, and like a reflex action his thick eyebrows darted like flies against his eyeballs.

'You must tell me more about this, Swami. I am extremely interested in this subject. My father, if he was alive today, would also be happy to hear what you say.'

'Your fadder – he dead?' Devan asked with a soft squeak in his voice, and he expected to see a frown appear on the other's face, but it didn't. Instead, Mr. Bhairam became sentimental and talkative and rolled his fingers into each other, forming a knot; all the while Devan looked at his hands as if he was a strange contortionist. Gocolram, eager not to be left out, mentioned how long Devan had been his guest and grinned genially.

'You've done well, Pandit,' said Bhairam. 'Next he must come to Georgetown.'

So many images danced before Devan's mind, that he couldn't think clearly anymore. Then Mr. Bhairam talked about the preparatory school for Hindu children, which he'd built in Georgetown. Devan forced himself to listen attentively, though his mind was whirling with all sorts of ideas, including that of bringing-up upright Hindu youths, and not least his son Jotish: the boy was never far from his thoughts.

Mr. Bhairam added, 'We must teach the young ones Hinduism. That's the main objective behind this preparatory. Too many of our young people are adopting Western ways here in Guiana. Our politicians are, too. Our fathers didn't come here for nothing, to make our children Christians and atheists. This has to stop!'

Devan loudly assented and Gocolram was not to be outdone. 'How soon you go start the preparatory?' asked Devan, getting off the mark before Gocolram this time.

'As soon as possible,' the voice of authority replied.

'You must get a good teacher then,' said Gocolram, unctuous in his smile, thinking of himself as a good choice since he'd secretly become fed up with Mahaica and wanted to live in Georgetown where most of the influential members of the League were. He wanted his own children to attend the best schools in the capital, those like Queen's College and Bishops High School – even though most of the teachers were Christians. But when he heard Mr. Bhairam say next, 'I would have some difficulty finding a good teacher,' Golcolram's heart sank somewhat, but being a positive thinker, he felt his chances were still good, he only had to wait for a while longer, and he winked at Devan and smiled in his customary way and then led Mr. Bhairam to the upper sanctum for refreshments. Later he would escort him to the Hindu temple.

Everyone wanted to pay their respects to Mr. Bhairam; Devan had never seen any thing like this: Hindus arriving in droves, bustling with excitement, chattering and eager, their faces smeared with sweet-smelling Yardleys talcum powder, their hair daubed with Mohini Hair Oil. They clustered about Mr. Bhairam and a dozen garlands were thrown round his neck, he smiling continually and laughing, delighting in all the attention. Devan also laughed, infected by the excitement. Gocolram nodded all the while, muttering confidentially in Devan's ear when he wasn't speaking to Mr. Bhairam. A garland was now thrown round Devan's neck, and one round Gocolram's, and more genial words flowed, more pleasant smells, flowers plentifully decorating the Mahaica temple, draped around pictures of the Hindu deities so that everything looked really festive and picturesque. Devan cast an eye at the women in their shimmering saris, their dark brown faces beaming, the younger, unmarried ones, slim-waisted and so beautiful; even the stouter women looked attractive as they jostled about the floor of the temple, each wanting a good seat to get a clear view of their benefactor and be seen by him as well, for everyone figured he'd become the new president of the All India League before long. The rumours continued to spread, and Devan nodded to each Hindu male who mentioned this to him now, acknowledging it as a long-gone conclusion, though Gocolram, still smiling, merely muttered a half-hearted approval as if he knew something no else did.

Devan looked immaculate in a longish robe, pure-white in colour with a red sash thrown round his neck against the hibiscus-ringed garland, and he breathed in heavily in barely suppressed excitement. Gocolram also looked splendid, though by no means as immaculate. In the background a harmonium played all the while, the notes rising occasionally, then becoming softer: all knew, of course, that the harmonium was Mr. Bhairam's favourite instrument.

Then it was time for Mr. Bhairam to speak. Getting up from the dais on which he had been sitting with folded legs, alongside Pandit Gocolram and Swami Devan, he surveyed the eager faces.

'I am a great lover of our Hindu music; it is such an important part of our tradition, you see. All Hindus love music, we have it in our blood, no?' He laughed, and the audience also laughed and tittered, the women in particular, and Mr. Bhairam continued, 'Next to the sitar the harmonium is my favourite instrument.' The music from the harmonium playing in the background revved up, then almost immediately fell to a low note; a palpable hush was in the air followed by a short applause, another acknowledgement of Mr. Bhairam.

'I am not a public speaker as you all know,' he continued. 'I am a man of action.' Agreeable laughter filled the short pause between these statements. Mr. Bhairam turned round and looked at Devan and Gocolram, then looked at his audience once more and wiped his forehead because of the intense heat which he'd begun to feel, and he continued with allusions to donations he'd made and intended to make, he being a man of action. He added, 'I've been hearing a great deal about Swami Devan – yes, Swamiji is an orator, I hear – a fine one too. The news gets around you know.' All eyes were on Devan now, though no one applauded, and Devan felt a dull torpor in the air and scratched his neck as if he felt a number of ants had suddenly crawled up it. Mr. Bhairam continued in an almost humorous way, 'Pandit Gocolram has been telling me about him ever since I arrived here, and maybe I will have the opportunity of listening to him myself, eh. Now, eh?' Again all eyes were on Devan, and it was if Mr. Bhairam didn't know what else to say and he took his seat once more alongside Gocolram on the dais.

Devan remained nonplussed for a second or two, and he sat looking at the audience, at all the Hindu faces before him, expecting him to get up. A vague sound, like a hiss, escaped from his throat, and Gocolram nudged him slightly and whispered, 'Here's your chance to impress Mr. Bhairam, Swami.'

'What?' cried Devan in another hiss. Then Mr. Bhairam turned and looked at him, and so did hundreds of other eyes, focusing on him, intently, like a thousand light bulbs. Devan knew he mustn't fail now, if he was ever to become a member of the All India League.

He rose. When he began speaking he was the Tarlogie pandit all over again, a thrill in his veins as the words flowed. It was as if he knew what had to be said and he talked about the need for the young people to be proud of their religion, for parents to instill in their children the right Hindu precepts – he was really thinking about Jotish again, his son's face firmly in his mind, his conviction growing stronger and stronger, the boy gathering flowers for him and seated next to him and chanting mantras. Devan beamed, exhorting his audience, telling them that too many of the young people were turning out to be rascals though he didn't tell them about the young people of his own Providence Village who had pelted bricks at his house, the rascals! If Hindu parents didn't do something before long, Guiana wouldn't be a place for East Indians anymore, it was doomed, atheism would take over; he appealed to sentiment, his voice rising and falling, a hush in his audience. Then, he spoke louder, with firmness, gesticulating:

'Our children are not taught Hindu culture in de schools, because dese schools are run by Christians, eh? We mus' stop this, because our heritage go be lost forever in Guiana. Now we mus' mek sure our young people, all our children, do not ignore our sacred religion, which is the oldest in the world, no? We go run our own schools, too, eh. *Acha!*' He glanced at Mr. Bhairam sideways, saw him smiling, and he felt renewed zest to talk about discipline next, quoting from the *Gita* once more to give texture to his words. But after a while his throat felt dry, and though he tried swallowing his own saliva, the words no longer came, and he wasn't sure what else he should say, try as he might. He stopped, and looked at everyone, and Gocolram started the first round of applause. As everyone else began applauding, Devan's head spun; he stood for a while longer before his audience, before the small microphone, like a man lost in a world all his own. Then he realised that Gocolram was standing next to him and leading him back to his seat and muttering to him and smiling, and Devan wasn't sure what he was saying but when he glanced at Mr. Bhairam he saw he too was also smiling.

Afterwards a crowd gathered round Mr. Bhairam, and Devan could not help thinking how a moment ago they had all been listening to him in an orderly fashion, but now (though a few came to him to shake hands) he was left standing all alone, as if it had been Mr. Bhairam who had given the speech.

Then Mr. Bhairam, still wiping his neck, said to him, 'It was a fine speech, Swami. You chose a good topic.' Gocolram, close by, assented quickly.

'Thank you,' said Devan.

'How would you like to become the first teacher of the Preparatory?' For a second Devan wasn't sure if he'd heard correctly, and he looked at Mr. Bhairam and thought he was going to frown heavily; then the offer fully dawned on him and he let out, 'Oh Blessed Deity,' which caused Mr. Bhairam to frown indeed, and Devan, only just stopping himself from clapping his hands, said in a very level voice:

'Of course, of course. I go become the first teacher.'

He said this in such a confident way, it was as if he knew all along that he'd be chosen. And Gocolram nearby, inwardly moaned and became downcast: for the first time he saw Devan as a threat, someone whom he shouldn't have brought out of obscurity. But he was resilient and he kept from showing his disappointment.

When Mr Bhairam had gone, Gocolram said to him: 'Bhai favour you well, Swamiji.'

The pandit continued to disguise his resentment by smiling beguilingly, and Devan tittered in an almost gloating way.

'I know, I know. Me gat to tank you for it, Pandit. You's older than me, he shoulda choose you instead.' Insincere as this comment was, Gocolram decided to dwell on it as if it were an absolute truth and he too tittered, though quietly.

'You really tink so, Swami?' He paused, looking at Devan as if he was seeing him for the first time, then added, 'Ah, Swami, me get old now. Bhai done well to choose you; you is an orator, no?' He said this as if he didn't believe in

Devan's oratorical skills, but he softened this by adding, 'You go mek one really good teacher. Prappa good one.'

'Indeed,' Devan said chirpily.

'Yes. Dat's why Bhai appointed you. The young people go learn under you.' Though Gocolram did not intend it, his tone was sceptical and ironic, and he laughed.

Looking at him, then down the street as if he would still see Mr. Bhairam's Mercedes, Devan said:

'Mr. Bhairam always mek up he mind so fast?'

Gocolram laughed heartily now without replying, then he hurried to be with his wife and children. That same night, lying beside his wife in bed, Gocolram muttered, 'Devan lucky you know. Bhai really favour him. He mek him de teacher.'

Mrs. Gocolram sulked at once, then she was on the attack: 'You shouldna bring he here! You should never have trust he!'

'Swamiji is guided by the power of God,' Gocolram attempted, trying to appease her.

She ignored this. 'You rememba how he accuse you of stealin' his provision, eh?'

Gocolram feared his wife's anger more than anything else, for it was usually followed by a period of silence and prolonged sullenness. He tried to appease her once more by saying that he was really an old man now and that teaching would be too much a burden for him. But Mrs. Gocolram scolded:

'You na too old fo' ride me at night though!' This caused Gocolram to turn slowly onto his side, and his wife added, 'Me glad he leaving anyway. He cause too much trouble in dis household. But is a shame Mr. Bhairam don' mek you the teacher!' Mrs. Gocolram's jaws clamped shut with a resounding thud. Gocolram, dourly facing the wall, merely murmured, more to himself than to her, 'You go see how quickly Swamiji will return to Providence. Teaching is hard work.'

Surprisingly, Mrs. Gocolram broke her silence and muttered, 'Mr. Bhairam go give he more favours. You see!'

The finality of her voice caused Gocolram to laugh hollowly against the wall, then he turned around to her side and tried putting his arm about her fat chest, which she resisted with a long-suffering sigh. Gocolram withdrew his arms quickly and again turned to the wall, dwelling on it as if he were looking at an abstract painting; he fell into a sound sleep before long.

He dreamt that he was standing with Devan at the train station, the train noisily pulling up, he shaking Devan's hand and saying with uncharacteristic loudness because of the noise, 'Na forget me, Swamiji. Rememba is me who bring you out of obscurity from Providence Village. Is me, eh?' Then he was laughing like a man who was delirious because he was thinking of Devan shaking Mr. Bhairam's hand in Georgetown and Devan increasing his influence and becoming a member of the All India League. He was still laughing as the train moved off; Devan was leaning out and waving, hair scattered before his eyes in the wind, as he moved farther away each second, leaving Mahaica for good it seemed, leaving all the ample gifts he was accustomed to receiving, and he, Gocolram, was laughing at him, at how disappointed he'd be from now on...

When Devan did leave on the coastal train, Gocolram seemed genuinely sorry to see him go. He stood on the platform, the train now barely visible in the distance, yet still seeing Devan's face. Then in the silence, the train no longer visible at all, Gocolram gazed vacantly at the Mahaica coastline, thinking that somehow he'd hear more about Devan before long. When he returned home the first thing he did was to gather his wife and children round him in the upper flat, burn incense for an full hour, and pray and chant. During all this time Mrs. Gocolram continued in her sullenness; it wasn't until a week later that she grew out of it, and very reluctantly too, Gocolram noted.

SEVEN

He had visited Georgetown once as a child and the images kept coming back to him vividly: the train rolling into the capital, his father seated next to him, and how different it was from Providence Village, and how thrilled he felt. He remembered how his father, an energetic but nervous figure in the city, had held his hand tightly as they walked along, and he had been amazed at the busyness of the traffic, people, the numerous shops, restaurants, stores. For his father, Georgetown was as far away as one could get from India. British Guiana was far enough, this place so close to the Orinoco and the Amazon, though Berbice, slow-moving, Indian populated and rice-growing, was not entirely dissimilar from village India. But Georgetown was entirely different. Cars honked, and his father held his hand even more tightly; everything was so hazardous. Devan, then eight years old, laughed from time to time at what he saw in the stores, the mannequins in the windows, and he kept asking questions, he wanted to know everything. Why were they here? Why didn't they live here instead of being in Providence Village where it was really dull? But Chattergoon pulled him closer and looked threateningly at him, as if to say that in Georgetown lived only the denizens of hell. 'Tek care, tek care,' urged his father, once more pulling him away as a cyclist careered close by, nearly running over Devan's legs, his father letting out, 'Oh *Bhagwan!*'

But Devan kept being fascinated by everything, despite the steamy heat that swirled and the traffic growing more hectic. And when the wind came again, tempering the heat, Devan breathed in hard and felt good, smelling the pleasant scent of the balsam and frangipani blossoms, these trees forming avenues almost everywhere they walked. But Chattergoon

– barefooted, as Devan was too – kept wondering why he had to come here, why the government had the right to find out all about him, he who had been born in India and not British Guiana. Did the formality of an official's questions necessitate his coming here – this place from where the radio stations beamed popular Indian songs to the villages, all across Berbice, Essequibo, to every outlying area of Demerara; this place where the British Governor lived, guarded as in a palace, soldiers and policemen about him? Devan remembered how his father had hurt his hand, so tightly had he gripped it, and how he had started crying, tired, his toes pinching him, wanting to pee as well. And Chattergoon had petulantly let out, 'Wha' wrang?' and when he had indicated his need, Chattergoon merely muttered, irascibly, 'You na see we in white people place, eh?' and he had had to tighten his legs and bear his pain, and concentrate on something else, on faces all around, white, black and brown and the many shades in between, Chinese faces as well, a whole new world to him.

As he got off the train now, these images faded, the present fully with him, Mr. Bhairam dominating his mind, Mahaica and Gocolram as if they had never existed. And where was Mr. Bhairam? Had he arrived too early? Would Mr. Bhairam keep his promise? Was it all a mistake? He said a quick prayer, looked around and began walking briskly, remembering the past once more; but his father wasn't with him this time and vaguely, quickly, an image of Jotish flitted across his mind. A car swung in almost at the paved curve close to him and Devan dashed closer to the sidewalk, convinced the driver was about to kill him. He began to have doubts. Was this where the brightest and best of the Hindus lived? Here indeed? Mumbling a prayer he walked on, looking left and right for Mr. Bhairam's beaming smile but seeing only indifference and hostility on the faces he passed, mocking his eagerness to meet Mr. Bhairam. Another car startled him, a cyclist nearly ran him over, and Devan dashed into the wall of Ho Sang's restaurant, his heart thumping excitedly. Someone shouted, 'Motherfucker!' At him? In a daze he looked around for Mr. Bhairam but saw only the departing cyclist laughing at him. He passed the door of D'Oliviera's Rum Shop and a drunk belched into his face; a gaudy-faced woman, who looked like a toucan, called out to him with her finger muttering, 'Fuckie-fuckie.' Devan uttered a mantra, the woman's surprising laughter throbbing in his ears. Then phrases from the *Gita* kept coming to his consciousness, the words strengthening him in the belief that all was destined... he had to be here now, to pursue greatness. *Acha!* He looked left and right, and as he became aware of the street's hazards, he was with Gautum Lall Chattergoon again, but in another moment it was he who was squeezing Jotish's hand and telling him to keep close to him, beware of the traffic, they would kill here! But the boy wilfully ran away from his grip, into the bewildering traffic... gone! Again he mouthed phrases from the *Upanishads*, and then, to his intense relief, he saw a few yards ahead of him Mr. Bhairam's Mercedes, evidently parked outside a store. He decided to wait right there, trying to compose himself for Mr. Bhairam as soon as he came out.

A few moments later he was sitting in the car, gliding down Lamaha Avenue with Mr. Bhairam, executive member of the All India League, telling him all about the houses they passed on the way, mostly owned by rich Hindus, many of whom were members of the League. Devan studied the patios with amazement, looked keenly at the edifices, the wide lawns, and he marvelled, his reaction so different from what he had felt before, now that he observed everything from the comfort and safety of the Mercedes with Mr. Bhairam's running commentary. His patron smiled continually and pressed on the gas. Devan also smiled, and from time to time grinned suitably, as he knew he must in order to appear unfailingly grateful.

They stopped in front of a ramshackle building a little way out of town in a seedy, run-down area. Was this the preparatory Mr. Bhairam talked about? The latter got out of the car, and Devan followed with bated breath. It was indeed the school, a large hall comprising the main teaching area and an adjoining room set aside for the teacher's living quarters. There was hardly any furniture in the building save for a greenish blackboard heavily frayed at the edges as if it had been retrieved from a rubbish dump. Devan's face fell, but when he saw Mr. Bhairam's frown, he remembered himself and immediately attempted a winning smile.

'There are plans ahead, Swami.'

'Plans?'

'Yes.' Mr. Bhairam looked at him in a deliberately scrutinising manner and Devan smiled, but wishing that Gocolram was around so he could confide in him his true feelings.

Mr. Bhairam added, 'The All India League has great plans for this school, you know. As soon as I become president of our illustrious organisation, it will be renovated; earlier, maybe.'

Again he looked peeringly at Devan, whose heart beat faster, his earlier gloom leaving him now as he saw prospects ahead, just as he'd thought, and he dismissed Gocolram from his mind.

Mr. Bhairam continued, 'You will have great responsibility here. This preparatory for Hindu youths will be a first in the country, mark my words, Swami.'

'Indeed.'

'It will be a model for preparatories we will build from coast to coast of Guiana. Yes, this country will be a different place, you understand?' Mr. Bhairam laughed as he became giddy with the vision in his mind, and Devan nodded and thought of such a school being built in Providence Village with his father, he figured, being the caretaker if not one of the teachers, old as he was. He looked at Mr. Bhairam who was still talking about the preparatories, and he felt a burning desire to start teaching at once. He mentioned this to his benefactor, who frowned, inauspiciously, and Devan wondered if he'd said the wrong thing.

In a grave tone, Bhairam murmured, 'You will have twenty children in your charge. You will start classes tomorrow. Today is rest day.'

'I go teach them well.'

'I have confidence in you, Swamiji. You're a fine orator, and they're bound to learn under your guidance,' though again Bhairam looked frowningly at him as if he didn't quite believe his own words.

They drove next down Vlissengen Road and before long arrived at what Mr. Bhairam described as his Villa, which Devan had heard about from the Mahaica pandit. Everything was happening so quickly; it was indeed the hand of fate at work, directing him. He wanted to tell the executive this, but wisely restrained himself. And the Villa was indeed a marvel, its unique fenestration, as Mr. Bhairam referred to it, being its most remarkable feature. At the very top storey was a tower which Devan said looked like a small temple itself, and Mr. Bhairam smiled because this was exactly what it was intended to be, such was its elegance. Flowers hung everywhere and when a refreshing breeze blew, the mansion seemed filled with a marvellous lightness of spirit as the leaves swayed on delicate stems, fanning the occupants; it seemed the ideal abode for Mr. Bhairam. Devan expressed his continuing delight, exaggerating his true feelings from time to time as if he had no control over his words; again he commented on the unique fenestration, which allowed abundant sunlight to filter in, to sweep into the main hall area, making it look larger than it actually was. 'It was Mrs. Bhairam's idea, these windows you know,' said Bhairam. 'She loves looking out, to see what's going on. It's her nature.'

Devan didn't smile, cryptic as he thought the remark was... thinking just then of Mrs. Gocolram. Would such a woman be here too? His heart sank a little, he no longer felt enthusiastic. Mr. Bhairam, observing this, was about to frown again, and Devan, catching himself quickly, said: 'Beautiful indeed, the windows – all.'

A talkative Bhairam now led him round the three flats of the Villa, and Devan repeated appropriate exclamations of delight, even though he was beginning to feel somewhat dizzy, not being used to climbing stairs in Providence. When they reached the tower, Mr. Bhairam's face really lit up, and Devan's similarly, thinking that this was the executive's pride of place. But the latter quickly said, 'Ah, you're yet to see my real delight, Swami.'

'Eh? What?'

Mr. Bhairam took Devan's hand as if he was a woman, his face still beaming, and Devan watched with keen interest, his curiosity increasing each second. Bhairam pointed through the window to a number of low-lying structures. 'My stables, Swami,' said Bhairam, still beaming.

'Stables?'

Mr. Bhairam's voice rose. 'Didn't the pandit tell you that I own the best race horses?'

At once Devan remembered. 'Yes-yes.'

'Come now, Swami – I will show you my jewel, my champion horse. He's really the fastest in the country.' And Bhairam, beaming and even looking youthful now, hurried out of the tower as if he despised it, leading Devan down the stairs at an almost break-neck speed. Devan panted behind Mr. Bhairam who kept talking about his horses – one in particular – while Devan spluttered with further appropriate exclamations. Finally they reached the stables and walked through the narrow enclosures with beams separating one bay from the other, the horses turning at every angle as if about to confront them, their hindquarters more often than not facing the visitors. Devan had never seen so many horses close up, and the smell of the stables made him hesitate; for a moment he wondered if it would have been more appropriate for Mr. Bhairam, as a Hindu, to keep cows, but he kept this thought to himself. Now and again a new horse turned and looked, he felt, at him in particular, but Mr. Bhairam was already leading him to the next.

They stood before the largest stable, and Mr. Bhairam, as if he was about to clap his hands in exultation, asked: 'Tell me what you think of my champion horse, Swami?' Devan looked at a sleek colt with large indomitable eyes like marbles, which looked back at him searchingly. Uneasily Devan blurted out, 'Magnificent animal!'

The horse snorted and the ground beneath Devan's feet throbbed; Devan stepped back at once, causing Bhairam to let out a short laugh.

'Ah, Destiny means no harm, Swamiji.'

'Destiny?'

'My horse. Surely you know its name.'

'Yes, indeed.'

Mr. Bhairam's look was less than congenial. Devan, like someone about to take off on a sprint, cried: 'Great horse! Fast horse!' Mr. Bhairam was pleased once more, and he turned his attention to the colt again, admiring it, slapping its neck and forehead, causing the horse to start a round of snorts, three or four times, each causing Devan to step back a few inches and wonder if this was some kind of sign – especially when the horse's eyes bulged at him; and he kept looking at the animal with an air of arrested astonishment.

'I see you're captivated by my horse, Swami,' Bhairam said.

Devan attempted another special smile, though with difficulty, for he was looking at Destiny fixedly once again and he only stopped doing this when Mr. Bhairam muttered, 'I have lots of enemies you know.'

'Enemies?'

'Yes, real ones, because of him maybe, and before long you will see them.'

'Oh?'

'Even among our Hindu brethren you will find them.'

Devan wasn't sure what to reply, and he looked away from Mr. Bhairam to the horse. Mr. Bhairam only stopped talking about his enemies when a tallish, sallow-skinned, saturnine-looking man of mixed race, maybe Portuguese and African, joined them; he stood like a ghost next to Mr. Bhairam and spoke quietly though determinedly.

'Meet my trainer, Jacob Athan.'

Devan looked from the man to the horse, then to the man again and muttered, dully: 'Trainer?'

'Yes. Of Destiny. Who else?' Mr. Bhairam was congenial again, and he explained to Jacob Athan, 'Swami Devan come from as far as ProvidenceVillage on the Corentyne–'

'Canje,' corrected Devan inaudibly, still looking at Athan.

'On the Corentyne they also have race-horses,' added Bhairam to his trainer, 'but not as good as we have here.' He laughed hollowly, while the trainer kept up his implacably solemn face.

Devan wondered about the trainer's mixed racial background. Why didn't Mr. Bhairam hire a Hindu to train his horses? He was contemplating this when the latter and Jacob Athan walked off to talk privately, leaving Devan alone. He turned his attention fully to Destiny. As if he willed it to happen, the horse just then snorted again. Devan muttered, 'Good sign or bad sign?' He waited for an answer and kept looking at it as it turned around a few times. Next he stretched out a hand, reaching the animal's forehead, and again the horse turned; Devan tried patting it and caressing its flank, and he laughed to himself as the horse remained still for a moment. He thought of Gosai's filly and how much he had loved currying it. Mr. Bhairam's voice interrupted his thoughts, 'Ah, I see you've taken a fancy to Destiny, Swami.'

Devan, starting, since he hadn't seen the executive return, nodded and looked for the trainer – who was walking away hurriedly. Mr. Bhairam seemed a little pale now, and he said – as they both looked at Athan's receding figure, 'He's leaving my service, you know.'

'Leaving?'

'Yes. It pains me indeed. But human nature, Swami.' Mr. Bhairam was prevented from saying more when a messenger came saying that Mrs. Bhairam was now expecting them in the Villa. And walking a little behind Mr. Bhairam, Devan wondered about the 'enemies' who might be around, and if Athan perhaps was one. Should he ask Mr. Bhairam this? But the latter was walking faster ahead of him, and Devan looked up at the windows of the Villa and just then felt a twinge of anxiety at meeting Mrs. Bhairam.

But Mrs. Bhairam was an affable, short, plump woman dressed in a sari of shimmering yellow; her skin had an almost lustrous texture; her face was distinctly oval and when she smiled it was as if her cheeks would stretch and overtake her ears. She kept up her affability all the while she talked to Devan, and the latter was forced to reflect that his view of women would have to include some exceptions – Mrs. Bhairam was one of a kind, naturally, she being the wife of Mr. Bhairam. She offered him sweetmeats, jelabies mostly, and smiled continually, and they were the most delicious Devan had ever tasted and he told her so as he swallowed the jelabies, chunks of them, almost whole.

Mrs. Bhairam watched him gulp and swallow again, and laughed.

Syrupy as the food was, Devan continued eating, because he realised now that he was really hungry.

'Have you seen Destiny?' she asked when they were alone for a while.

'Yes – splendid haas.'

'Bhai is always pleased to hear that. But tell me, why is he so upset?'

'Upset?' Devan turned and looked at Mr. Bhairam a few feet away and stopped munching. Indeed, Mr. Bhairam looked very pale, and he offered an explanation: 'Oh, I think it's because of the trainer.'

'Jacob Athan?'

'Yes, I think they had an argument.' He lowered his voice, and Mrs. Bhairam came closer to him, a whiff of her perfume wafting up his nostrils even as she looked dour now and a little pale herself. Devan attempted a smile but was prevented from carrying it out when she said, 'He isn't leaving again, is he?'

Before Devan could answer, she rushed to her husband and repeated the questions, a look of abject pain on her face – as Devan unhappily noticed close by. 'I am afraid so,' said Mr. Bhairam.

'But the October races are only six weeks away, Bhai.'

'I know,' Mr Bhairam replied, and he frowned in such a heavy manner that it seemed his entire face was overtaken by the frown. Then, both he and Mrs. Bhairam looked at Devan who was slowly wiping away the sticky syrup smeared at the corners of his mouth as if it was a strange resin that had somehow formed on its own, and he didn't know what else to do in their presence.

EIGHT

Nine children showed up on the first day of classes, and Devan looked at them forlornly for a while, not sure what he should do. The children tittered, bemused at the odd figure sitting before them, refusing to be cowed as Devan intended would happen. They tittered a little more loudly. Devan shifted uncomfortably in his seat as he copied their names and repeated them to himself slowly. Then he asked them their ages, which ranged from six to sixteen; again he watched them as they waited restlessly for him to begin teaching. He got up and stood before the blackboard and remembered his own schooldays, how the teacher often wrote up words for the pupils to copy. Looking at the *Gita*, he drew a few words from it onto the board, and ordered, 'Copy dat!' The children giggled.

Devan looked at them and for a second thought of giggling himself, not sure what to do. Then he sat down at his small wooden table, the *Gita* still open before him. He heard more of their giggles, louder this time. Looking up from the *Gita* to the words on the board and to them again, he murmured, 'They never go learn,' and thoughts of Jotish drifted into his mind. He felt pained, and he looked at his charges and sighed loudly. One of those who had heard him sniggered loudly in response. 'Rascal,' Devan let out under his breath and looked searingly at them; they looked back at him, impishly, and Devan lowered his eyes to the *Gita* again. He decided to dismiss the class for the rest of the day after only one hour, the longest in his life. 'Go home,' he shouted to them as they rushed out, sighing when they were gone, 'Maybe more come tomorrow.'

The drab walls of his room greeted him like a prison, ready to squeeze him into a state of abject claustrophobia. He closed his eyes tightly and meditated, the hurly-burly atmosphere of the classroom fading; he felt composed, ordered, far removed from the incorrigibility of children's nature. He smiled, eyes still closed. Now he concentrated on what he would teach the next day, words from the *Gita*, a jumble of phrases racing across the blackboard, his mind. He began seeing himself as a teacher constantly being approved by Mr. Bhairam; he was saying, with eyes still closed, I go teach them well. I will, you go see, and he was smiling and the executive was nodding in approval.

The next day the same number of children showed up and they set about drawing fanciful objects in their workbooks. Devan, hands akimbo, bawled out to them, 'Copy the words on the blackboard – copy dat!' His voice was intimidating only in his own ears, and the children sniggered. Devan threw up his hands in dismay. After two hours of this, he decided he'd had enough and sent them home. Inside his room he grumbled, 'Is a hard life being a swami and a teacher.' Then he decided to meditate, folding his legs and conjuring up the image of Mr. Bhairam once more. This made him feel better.

The next day Mr. Bhairam showed up just when Devan was about to think that the executive had completely forgotten him; he smiled a welcome.

'How are you getting along, Swami?' Mr. Bhairam asked.

'Hard work to be a teacher,' he complained.

Mr. Bhairam looked at his class of ten faces, each one now obedient, cooperative, docile, and he said, 'You're a fine orator, you will inspire them in no time.'

'Yes,' Devan agreed, pleased with this vote of confidence, but when he looked at his charges his zeal diminished. Mr. Bhairam shifted his attention to the *Gita* on Devan's table and added, 'So you've been reading that, eh? You must teach it to them. You must, Swami.' And Devan agreed, even though he knew the impossibility of this task, especially with children who drew horses and trees instead of copying the words on the board. And Mr. Bhairam added, 'You see, the Muslims, their children know the *Koran* by heart; they do you know.' The executive looked grave, and once more he turned his attention to the students, who responded with equally solemn faces.

As soon as Mr. Bhairam had left, the class became as noisy as before. Devan shouted for them to be quiet, then in a clear voice he ordered them once more to copy the Hindi alphabet. Next, loudly, he asked them to repeat the words to him, believing that they would learn by rote; but the children fidgeted and groaned as they grew tired, and one or two – the very youngest – fell asleep. Devan, remembering Mr. Bhairam's words, murmured, 'Learning is difficult,' and sat at his table and stared blankly at the open *Gita*, the Hindi letters like weird insects running about before him, then alternately remaining in abject stillness.

Mr. Bhairam took him on another visit to the Villa and Devan was immensely pleased; before long he found himself chatting with Mrs. Bhairam whom he liked more and more; he figured she liked him too, they were so congenial in each other's company. She was so charming the way she laughed and then demurely covered her mouth with a sleeve of her sari; but he soon discovered that she was confident and outgoing, unlike any other East Indian woman he knew. For the first time he began to believe that women were God's special creation. The more he chatted with Mrs. Bhairam the more he felt this. It was from her too, since he had gained her confidence, that he first learnt about the imminent renovations of the Preparatory. The League, he also learnt from her, was getting really interested in the project, at Mr. Bhairam's behest; they were beginning to make contacts with India about the education of the young.

'India, eh?' Devan asked.

'Yes, yes, Swami. It is where our parents came from, no?' She tittered a little, not unlike the children in his class.

'Oh, yes,' he agreed, and he laughed to himself because a vision of a direct link between Guiana and India suddenly excited him. 'It go be like a little India here, eh?' he asked rhetorically, his mind still working at top speed. 'Me go see India wid me own eyes right here, eh?' he added.

'Acha, Swamiji. India and Guiana will be like one.'

'Yes,' Devan nodded vigorously, almost clapping his hands as he added, 'the Preparatory go be the place fo' everyone to attend. EVERYONE!' He noticed how wide her eyes opened. Was it because of what he said? He wasn't sure, and as he started talking at a rapid pace about how his teaching was coming along – it was his mission in life, wasn't it? – he looked for her approval; but she merely watched him, whether admiringly or distantly he couldn't tell, though when she laughed out loudly she seemed to be mocking him, her eyes devoid of affection. He wondered about this all the way back to his room, and kept thinking about it all night. He concluded that she meant well. How could he think negative thoughts about her? Impossible!

The next morning he awoke to the sounds of loud banging outside, and he knew at once that the renovations had begun. Rushing to the window, he saw a group of carpenters hammering at the walls as if they were about to tear down every building in the block. 'God be blessed,' he muttered, his hands to his ears. 'At last they building a new school,' and the hammering resounded so heavily that far a moment he became genuinely afraid. When the children came that morning he cried out to them, 'Go home, you rascals! No teaching today! Go home an' learn Hindi! Learn about the *Gita*.' The children fled.

For three weeks the renovations continued, and each morning Devan got up and muttered, 'God be blessed,' and sometimes he thought of Mrs. Bhairam in the same breath, imagining her in her sari and the affable way she talked and laughed. Before long he was back at the Villa, to be close to Mrs. Bhairam. But it was Mr. Bhairam who was waiting for him – to take him round to the stables, in particular to look at Destiny, the champion horse: to talk incessantly about the coming races in one breath and about man's evil nature in another. Then back to the Villa, and Devan was introduced to other members of the All India League who came to visit. Sitting in a corner Devan listened to the talk of horses intermixed with discussion about the League's work, new ideas, new plans, about increasing the influence of Hinduism in the country. And the more familiar he became with these guests, the less overwhelmed Devan was by that august organisation. Yet his yearning to join them increased tenfold: he didn't want to be an outsider any longer.

He was introduced to a short, dapper, tweed-smelling merchant, Ganesh Lall, who was now the most frequent visitor to the Villa. Lall had a beguiling laugh all his own, and to Devan he said, 'Ah, Swami, you must consider yourself to be the first teacher of the Preparatory, eh? Bhai is very impressed with you, too, no?'

Devan thanked the merchant, and watched him with interest, though not without some suspicion.

'I hear you are well-known in Mahaica also,' added Lall.

Devan was pleased at this recognition. 'Yes-yes,' and warmed towards him with a smile.

'Fine orator, too, no?'

Devan's liking for Lall increased, and the merchant added, 'Mr. Bhairam always needs orators.' But Lall didn't smile now as Devan expected him to, even though he tapped Devan on the shoulder, leant forward, and muttered in his ears, in a half-conspiratorial fashion: 'Yet not for the children, Swamiji – but for the coming elections, eh.'

'Elections?'

'Don't you know dat the League elections are not far off?'

'Oh yes.' Devan managed a frown.

'Ah,' Lall laughed, 'don't be worried. It's the rural Hindu vote Mr. Bhairam needs more than any of the others. He sure to become president of our organisation. He'll be at the helm, you will see!' There was something about the finality in Lall's voice which made Devan look suspiciously at him, even though Lall's words expressed his own sentiments, but when Lall assured him that with Mr. Bhairam as president he would have no trouble being a member of the elite League, he dismissed all negative thoughts and in exhilaration clapped Lall affectionately on the shoulder. Lall reciprocated the bonhomie and affection.

The opening of the Preparatory was a big affair, attended by some of the wealthiest Hindu merchants, doctors and lawyers and their wives and daughters, dressed in their newest saris, glittering with jewellery. Everyone talked and laughed, the women mixing freely with the men, and then they looked around at the renovated building with expressions of awe. Devan, in a long white shirt, hair vaselined and combed straight back to give him a sleek appearance, also mingled, trying to be sociable, but each time he tried to engage someone in conversation he found that they drifted away from him before long, always crying out a hello to someone else a few feet away. Devan, left standing alone, focused his attention again on the women, most of whom wore lipstick and reeked of heady perfume: they looked like pictures of women in foreign magazines, he thought, and he kept being amazed at how confident they were as they talked boldly with the men and sometimes laughed loudly too. After a while he unconsciously fell back on his habit of phrenological speculation, concentrating on everyone's foreheads, but nothing seemed to match his prescription of what really important people's faces ought to be like. Dismissing phrenology, he again looked at the women, slim-waisted, elegant and attractive. It was a pity Mrs. Bhairam hadn't come for he felt the urge to talk to her now. Lall came up and put a hand on his arm and, chewing salted nuts with rodent-like zeal, he pointed to someone in a knot of guests, a frail-looking man of medium height and soft, though becoming, features. 'Dat's Nakeram Harresh, Swamiji. Tek good note of him; he is the outgoing president of the League.'

Devan concentrated on the president, whose photograph he had seen in the newspapers once or twice; he wasn't impressed by his living presence and was about to tell Lall this when the latter disappeared to be with another crowd of merchants, leaving Devan once more to himself. He watched Lall with his coterie for a minute as he talked loudly, waving his arms incessantly and smiling all the while with everyone. Devan shifted his attention back to Nakeram Harresh, observing the ladies gathered about him making a fuss, playfully so, and how he chatted with them, now and again stretching out a petal of a hand, the tendrils of his fingers coiled about the delicate ladies' waists as he engaged them in further laughter, then, alternately, in serious conversation. So absorbed was he with this picture that he didn't realise someone was standing close to him, addressing him in a familiar voice:

'You mus' na tink he is the real force in the League, Swamiji.'

Devan turned around and saw Pandit Gocolram before him, and they embraced and exchanged compliments like old friends. 'How d'you enjoy teaching?' asked Gocolram.

'Dem learn well,' Devan replied.

'I am happy to hear it, Swami. Soon they learn better now, eh.' Gocolram pretended to look around at the large building with the wider hall area and the spacious siderooms for workshops, commenting on them as if he was an architect who had reached the height of his profession; and Devan listened keenly and smiled one of his ingratiating smiles – by now he had an array of them for different occasions. Then Devan asked, 'Who is de real force in the League, Panditji?'

Gocolram breathed in heavily, his gaze stretched out across the gathering, deliberately taking his time, 'Why, Sarwan Singh of course.'

'Sarwan Singh?'

'No one tell you, Swamiji?'

Gocolram forced a look of surprise, then happily smiled as he watched Devan pass a nervous flutter of a hand over his vaselined head; Devan wondered why Lall hadn't told him this before.

Gocolram filled in the details, again taking his time in

order to draw out the most effect. 'Singh one brilliant lawyer; God really bless Hindu people, Swami.'

'Brilliant, eh?' Devan's heart sank a little, and he fidgeted even more, as Gocolram noted to his satisfaction.

'Yes. Dey go be a prappa struggle for power in the elections. Many think Sarwan Singh go defeat we own Mr. Bhairam.'

'It cyan' happen!' Devan burst out, his voice going up an octave.

But Gocolram chuckled nonchalantly, and Devan – as if his life depended on it – cried once more, 'Mr Bhairam mus' win!'

'Me hope so. Then it'll be easy fo' you to become a member of the League, eh?' Gocolram taunted, winking at him in a friendly way, then, pointing to some of the other prominent members of the League present, proceeded to give a detailed description of the profession each was engaged in and the extent of their influence. Devan couldn't help being amazed by Gocolram's knowledge and, as if he was seeing him for the first time, instinctively studied the pandit's forehead in phrenological fashion. But he was prevented from dwelling more on this when a slight rustle arose among the guests clustered at the entrance and a tallish, dynamic-looking figure walked in. In a dark suit, Sarwan Singh exuded an agreeable but austere air and he nodded with a grace mixed with a becoming arrogance. Devan kept looking at him almost spellbound, especially at the way he twirled his well-trimmed moustache. He shifted his attention to Mr. Bhairam a few yards away who seemed distinctly shorter in contrast and not as impressive-looking as before. Somewhat confused Devan looked at Gocolram, who was smiling widely. 'You see what I mean, Swami,' he said.

Devan looked at Bhairam again; he seemed heavy in the middle in contrast to Singh's dashing figure. Gocolram, realising what was going through Devan's mind, muttered: 'You mustn't worry, Swami.'

'Eh?'

'Worry.' Gocolram made a short cackling sound, adding: 'You bound to become a member of the League; but first–' he paused again and in a lowered, conspiratorial tone added, 'we must mek sure Bhai wins.'

'Yes, we must,' Devan agreed quickly. 'He must win at all cost.'

They were prevented from further discussion of the upcoming elections when prayers started the day's ceremony; then Mr. Harresh, in a clear, mellifluous voice, made a few announcements and apologised for the absence of the treasurer and that therefore a financial report pertaining to the renovation costs could not be read out – which produced a few sarcastic groans from the audience. Nakeram Harresh wetted his thin lips in mild embarrassment, then in a louder tone said that the report would be mailed out to all the financial members. Harresh continued, showering praise on Mr. Bhairam for initiating the idea of the Preparatory and Devan began to feel better as Mr. Bhairam took a slight bow, unimpressive though it was. Harresh praised Mr. Bhairam's commitment to Hinduism in Guiana, a land far away from their real homeland of India. No one applauded, though Devan was on the verge of doing this, until Gocolram rested a cautionary hand on his. Together they listened to Harresh again as he wetted his lips and added, 'It is to our young people that we must pay full attention. They must have a first-class Hindu education with the best teachers available.'

Devan's heart beat faster, for he thought his name would be mentioned. But it wasn't and, almost chuckling, Gocolram whispered, 'Na lose faith, Swami. You go get yuh reward later.'

Mr. Bhairam now rose to speak, and Devan watched expectantly as his benefactor apologised for not being a public speaker and then repeated some of the things Mr. Harresh had already said, causing some good-natured laughter from the women. Mr. Bhairam also laughed, then tried to assume an unbecoming seriousness as he concluded, 'There is great good to be gained by knowing our sacred culture, the first in the world because of the *Vedas*. A school is the best place to teach it and to make sure that our young people become staunch Hindus.' Devan's heart beat faster, for he felt he was the one speaking, even though he would have gesticulated once or twice; again he glanced at the women as Mr. Bhairam continued haltingly, as if he didn't know what else to say, then he blurted out in an almost comical way that the idea for the Preparatory came to him while he was playing the harmonium, and then quickly, but vaguely, alluded to the coming elections and took his seat.

The entire speech lasted five minutes, and brief applause followed, the women wearing the heaviest lipstick clapping the longest. Gocolram, applauding in a perfunctory way with his knuckles, said to Devan, 'He shoulda mention yuh name, Swami.' His tone was regretful, and it caused similar sentiments to go through Devan.

Sarwan Singh now walked to the platform, and how confident he looked. He didn't begin with an apology, and he enunciated his words well, pausing appropriately for the maximum effect, and when his voice rose for emphasis it carried an appealing resonance. Everyone listened with rapt attention as he talked about Hinduism in Guiana, with references to Hinduism in neighbouring Trinidad – a place he had been to – and the need for Hindus everywhere in the region to unite. Loud applause followed. Singh next talked about the school:

'It must play an important role in fostering an upright Hindu youth in Guiana so that all Christians and Muslims – Guianese as we all are – will see the value of our religion through the behaviour of our youths. They must not become communists and atheists or vagrants, and be a disgrace to our heritage.' His voice rose, 'This school, brothers and sisters, must be made to surpass every other school in Guiana and in the entire Caribbean; it must have the highest standards at all time, with the best qualified teachers; this will not be hard to achieve, and our motto should be that the Georgetown Preparatory will be a model for all. Hinduism as a way of life must prevail, and our African brothers and sisters must join with us as we forge a collective goal, a common unity among all our peoples, far away as we are from India. We must avoid strife and division, for we are all God's children, and this Preparatory will make sure these things are taught in the spirit of our noble religion.'

Sarwan Singh spoke in this forthright and high-minded way for another half-an-hour, growing in his audience's estimation as they listened to him eagerly. Watching him Devan grew envious, and when he turned and saw Mr. Bhairam listening keenly, his envy grew to resentment. When Singh began talking about the coming elections, his voice resounding like a true leader's, Devan hated him, and when he looked at Gocolram and saw he was nodding constantly with approval, Devan's disgust was complete. The applause that followed the end of the speech was deafening; even Mr. Bhairam was clapping. Gocolram muttered, 'Brilliant speech, Swamiji.'

'Yes,' Devan replied, not knowing what else to say.

For the rest of the afternoon Devan noticed how everyone kept congratulating Singh on his speech; even Lall, and Devan – reluctantly – found himself doing the same. Gocolram, just before he left, again reminded Devan, 'Is a pity no one mentioned your name, Swami. Just think, it might mek it easy fo' you to become a member, na? After all, you is the first teacher!'

NINE

Devan sat at his desk, almost at the same spot where Sarwan Singh had made his speech, and the latter's words, his gestures, came flooding back to him and he could not stop thinking about the favourable contrast he had made with Mr. Bhairam. He frowned a few times, the students watching him, including the ten others who had joined the original nine. These new ones were older-looking; Devan felt sure they wouldn't learn. They glared at him, as he thought about Singh's emphasis on discipline, on the Preparatory being a model school. Unconsciously he winced, and he thought he would teach them Hindu ethics: this would be the basis for a solid Hindu education. Unconsciously he grinned. The boys at the back watched him, intrigued, and they too grinned.

Parents began coming to the school now, wanting to find out more about Devan. While the children copied words of ethics from the blackboard, Devan regaled the parents with stories about his oratorical skills, and they watched him with intrigue and interest, but wanted to know about his qualifications.

Devan looked sad for a moment, then quickly said he'd been studying Hinduism all his life, he'd been marked out to do just this; they should be glad to have someone like himself as the teacher at the Preparatory. The parents looked dubious, and wanted to know about his family and where he came from. They had never heard of Providence Village. Was it really in Berbice? And where was his wife? Devan told them that she was with his parents, that Tara believed in his meditating and studying; she really did. It was his destiny to be the teacher, to instruct the young about Hindu ethics. Again they looked at him, a little sceptically. Devan told them about the Mahaica Hindus, how they really appreciated him. He grinned and watched them go. He would wait until the next day. And the next: he would be patient.

One morning when he entered the main hall he found the children noisier than usual. 'Quiet, you devils!' he let out, looking at the older ones at the back. There was silence for a while, and Devan looked anxiously at them, still simmering with rage. Gandhi's *Art of Living* lay before him on the table and he opened it wondering which passage to start with. The core of ethical behaviour came from India; it had to be Gandhi, who else? Still looking at the boys, he hoped that before long they would take home a code of ethics to their parents, especially the ones who asked about his beginnings in Providence Village.

But the noise continued and, after a while, Devan looked up from his book, glowering. 'Shut up, you monkeys!' he fired back at them, getting up that instant and walking to the back of the class, then returning in almost military fashion to the front again. 'All ahyou are monkeys,' he repeated, unable to suppress his anger.

'We en no monkeys,' one of the older youths retorted.

Devan frowned.

'Eh? If not monkey, then you baboon!'

'We're not baboons either,' came a further retort, and laughter followed from the entire class: everyone now looking at him, at the intensity of his expression. Devan, unable to stand this impertinence any longer, grabbed a whip which he had hidden in his desk and lashed out, whop-whop-whop! One boy screamed and then bolted out of the hall, with Devan taking after him still lashing out blindly and shouting: 'Baboon! Monkey! Come back here! Come back, rascil!'

But the boy was too fast for Devan and on the way out he shouted: 'I telling my father: I will – he a docta!'

The word 'docta' made Devan freeze in his tracks and he watched the boy sprinting away along the brick road to the main highway. And he wondered if the boy's father was a member of the All India League, and if all the others at the back also had fathers who were members of the League. Why hadn't he thought of this before? A little meekly, he returned to his class, set them to practising the Hindi alphabet and, without looking at his charges, he sat at his desk concentrating heavily on *The Art of Living*. Even when the noise rose, he didn't look up from his book.

Then once in a while he raised his head, hoping he would see the one who'd escaped. He also expected the doctor would arrive at any moment, and he grew nervous. He turned the page of the book, unable to concentrate any longer.

That afternoon he kept his charges in class longer than usual, making them copy down passages from *The Art of Living*, still hoping the escapee would show up, that he had not gone home. And when he finally dismissed class at about six o' clock because he grew tired of sitting at his table, he went straight to his room and started a serious bout of meditation For a while he imagined himself back in his old room in Providence village, praying, meditating – no teaching, no one to worry him. Then a noise broke his concentration, and opening his eyes he muttered in a self-consoling way, 'Well, he rascil anyway,' and remembered the boys at Providence Village, how they had teased and tormented him.

A few days later Sarwan Singh visited the school. Devan at once sensed trouble. As Singh came closer to his table and stretched out a stiff hand, Devan jumped up and blurted out, 'If you come to find out about the boy–'

'What boy, Swami?'

While the children laughed derisively at his nervous behaviour, Devan reluctantly reported the incident, emphasising that the boy had been insolent, rude, had called him funny names and was indeed a rascal.

'What funny names?'

'Baboon. Monkey–'

The lawyer burst out laughing, then became grave, and looked at Devan as if he was seeing him for the first time. 'Did you punish him?'

'He ran away before I could.'

'I see.'

Then the lawyer went and chatted with the children at the back of the class, looking at their books from time to time, all to Devan's chagrin, for he feared what Singh might see: drawings of houses and trees. But the lawyer lifted up one book and showed Devan the pictures of monkeys and baboons, and again laughed. He came up to Devan once more. 'I have news for you, Swami.'

'News?'

'A Board of Governors has been formed.'

'Board of Gov'nors? What for?'

'To be in charge of the running of the Preparatory. Remember, we must have high standards.'

Devan looked at the lawyer twirling his moustache as if he was pulling at wires at the sides of his face, and it seemed as if the wires were growing longer and longer the more he watched them, and he closed his eyes for a moment, a large frown appearing on his face. The children thought he'd suddenly become ill and again they sniggered.

'From now on,' said Singh, 'all disciplinary matters will be investigated by the Board. I will have to investigate this incident with the boy; I am sure you understand.'

'Yes,' said Devan, still looking at the wires on Singh's face.

'We can't allow this to continue.'

'Yes,' Devan agreed meekly. When Singh had gone, he examined each workbook in the class, starting with the boys at the back and, just as he expected, they had all drawn pictures of monkeys and baboons with human faces. Thinking the faces were all his, he bolted the door so no one could escape, took out his whip – as he recalled his teachers did to him at Providence Village – and lashed out: whop-whop-whop.

'Blasted Board of Gov'nors! Blasted children!' he shouted. 'Go home an' learn Hindi, you rascils!' He opened the door and pointed outside, and the children, as if they were running from a demon, fled shouting at the tops of their voices, 'Baboon, Monkey!'

The next week Devan started classes earlier, and kept them later than usual, hoping he would impress the Board of Governors. The children grumbled and sulked and before long Devan noticed that absences were growing and, contrary to what he hoped, the children became noisier. When some of the parents visited again, they commented on the noise. It was even suggested that he should have help.

'Yes, indeed,' said Devan, beaming, the idea appealing to him. He wasted no time in drafting a letter to the Board of Governors, smiling to himself as he licked the envelope, convinced that before long he'd get help. How could Singh refuse him? He mentioned that he had forty-five students now. Yes, the letter would do the trick.

A few days later Mr. Bhairam arrived. Devan rushed to him, thinking his benefactor had come to announce the good news. Help was at hand. But Mr. Bhairam's eyebrows looked as if they wanted to reach his lower lip, and Devan stopped in his tracks, muttering in a disconsolate way that he'd written to the Board of Governors about his problem. He looked at Mr. Bhairam, his mind seething with anxiety.

'It has already been taken care of, Swami.'

'Already?' Devan was about to start smiling. Bhairam, however, quickly added: 'A new teacher has been appointed. A new principal. He will take your place.' Devan drew in his breath in the beginnings of a groan. 'You must understand,' Mr. Bhairam added hastily, 'it's not my doing. I am disheartened by this move.

'After all me done for dis school,' Devan lamented; and looking at his class, for the first time he thought he would miss the children.

'The new principal is from India,' said Bhairam.

'From India, eh?' Devan couldn't help marvelling at this.

'Yes. We're fortunate to get him in fact. He's Sri Aurobindo Ghose. Bachelor of Arts. Sanskrit scholar.'

Devan, impressed though he didn't want to show it,

repeated Aurobindo Ghose's qualifications as if he was about to start chanting a mantra, then he blurted out: 'It's Sarwan Singh's doing! I know it!'

Mr. Bhairam moved back a few inches at this outburst, and he frowned even more heavily, then said: 'How would you like to stay at the Villa?'

'At the Villa?' Devan couldn't believe his ears, and once more thoughts about his mission in life came to him. 'Yes-yes. Thank you,' and he grinned from ear to ear and looked at his charges and figured he could manage without them.

'You could help me with the horses,' Mr. Bhairam said.

'Horses, eh?' Gosai's filly flashed into his mind but he looked perplexedly at Mr. Bhairam for a second, then continued smiling like a man who was nonplussed and relieved at the same time.

'The October meeting is close by. Besides, Jacob Athan has left my service for good, Swami.'

Devan didn't reply; he merely looked at his benefactor with a puzzled air.

When Mr. Bhairam left, Devan continued thinking about Athan, someone whom he hadn't really liked, whom he'd been happy had left. But himself as the trainer? Was it possible? And he thought of Mr. Bhairam's favourite horse, the animal's eyes, the way Destiny snorted at him. 'Good sign or bad sign?' he asked out loud. The children heard him, and looked up wondering, some laughing. But Devan wasn't really conscious of them now, and he gravely wondered about the supernatural force guiding his life. The children merely thought he was funny and laughed louder.

TEN

Devan occupied a room in the lower flat of the Villa, not much bigger than the one in the Preparatory. Now he believed he would have all the time in the world to contemplate and meditate, to pray and chant hymns. He wouldn't have to get up early in the morning to teach anymore. Here was where he would fit in, would really prove himself. And in his favourite lotus posture, closing his eyes, allowing new thoughts, new sensations to go through him, he breathed in heavily and slowly let out the air to his satisfaction. '*Ohm*,' he murmured, in almost silent incantation. Again he uttered the name of God, the Omniscient, the Creator of the Universe, but just when he felt he was being pulled into a dark, unfathomable area of his mind, the deepest layer of consciousness, he heard the sound of horses neighing. At once he opened his eyes, alarmed. It was Destiny, he thought angrily, for the sound disturbed him. 'Damn the horses,' he muttered, 'Damn them, damn them all!' He tried closing his eyes again and concentrating, but it was no use; nothing would bring him back to the layer of consciousness he had been on the point of entering. Instead he pictured Destiny, the horse's large eyes growing wider each moment, and he was unaccountably disturbed.

'Damn them, damn them all,' he cried out loudly, just as Mrs. Bhairam was passing by, eager to see that he was well.

'Is everything alright, Swami?' she asked.

He opened his eyes wider, as if he was experiencing a vision, her sari shimmering before him, her eyes arresting his. He studied the shape of her body but quickly chided himself. The senses must not get the better of him, never; it was his life's work to control the senses.

'Nothing wrong,' he replied, trying to gather his composure, getting up at once, believing more and more that she was the perfect hostess. She laughed, came closer to him, observing him, more intrigued than ever. 'Bhai told me about your father, Swami,' she said sentimentally. She felt bored and in need of company because he husband was away. She didn't really care for the other Georgetown Hindu women, and she didn't really mind Swami Devan's mannerisms, she had a tolerant nature. 'Your father travelling on the same ship with his father – what a coincidence!'

Devan forced himself to concentrate on a ship in the Atlantic Ocean packed with Hindus, as African slaves had been in the slave-trade. There was hardly any room for them below deck, and they often stifled from the lack of air. Waves were lashing on all sides, the ship canting, and his father was thinking of his death even though the lure of Guiana was still in his mind. And he imagined a dozen other ships, all following one another, packed with coolies, cheap labour for the sugar estates... Slavery was done with? A jabber of Hindi words, prayers, incantations, all uttered in dire fear, to the accompaniment of waves crashing, some rising up like hills. Mrs. Bhairam continued, 'Our people really suffered a lot, all because of the British.'

'The British?' he asked, since he'd never really thought of this term in relation to the few white people he'd seen in Georgetown or the white overseers from the sugar estates at Blairmont or Rosehall whom he'd seen from a distance, riding by on their fast motor-cycles and in their land-rovers. He knew nothing about such people, and wasn't sure if they were Christians or atheists – they were definitely not Hindus. All he knew was that it was under the white overseers that some of the Providence villagers worked as labourers on the neighbouring sugar estates. His own father had worked in the shovel gang for many years until the arthritis it caused had forced him to work on his own as a small farmer on a piece of land he'd bought with his meagre life savings. The British? Mrs. Bhairam used this term so casually that he appraised her afresh, concentrating on the shimmering of her sari, as if intelligence itself coruscated from it.

Just when he wanted Mrs. Bhairam to continue, she shifted talk to her husband. 'Bhai has so much to do now, especially since his trainer left. He's so busy, and the League elections too, and the October race meeting coming up...' She threw her hands up in a gesture of hopelessness and looked at him for solace.

'Have faith in God,' he murmured, moving closer to her and inhaling her Yardleys perfume, and when he expected her to retreat a few inches, she remained still, smiling.

'True, Swamiji, I will put my trust in God.' Then, without waiting any further she hurried away from him, her silk sari swishing as she walked up the stairs to the main dwelling on the second floor; and Devan once more struggled with his resolve not to dwell on the shape of her body, and he chided himself even as he heard the swishing of the sari deep in his ears. Closing his eyes and resisting the urge to think about Mrs. Bhairam again, her oval-shaped face, her grace and charm, he tried to concentrate on Chattergoon instead, the ship rolling and his father crying out for *Bhagawan*. Then Lachandai's face came to him; she too had sailed in that ship, and how young she'd been, but he'd never asked her about it and no one had ever told him, female as she was, insignificant. He closed his eyes, strong in his resolve, and Tara's face came up next, she completely supplanting Mrs. Bhairam, and he recalled the first years of their marriage and how agreeable her body was to him and how well she'd proved in bearing him children. But then Tara and the children were on the ship, waves lashing the sides. They were drowning. *Oh God, help them! Oh Bhagawan!* The ship canting on the horizon, drifting away, further away from him, and where were they going? Where were they returning to? Shangrila... India... leaving him alone in the wasteland of Guiana?

Mr. Bhairam took him on another tour of the stables, this time to meet the stable-boys; Devan felt anxious even though Mr. Bhairam was at his most congenial, and told him, 'Make sure they do as you command them. They have been with me a long time, especially Punam.'

'Punam?' Devan repeated, dwelling on the Hindu-sounding name, and beginning to lose his anxiety.

'He's the most reliable, you see,' Mr. Bhairam added. 'That's what Athan used to tell me.' He chuckled a little as if he was embarrassed to mention the former trainer's name. 'But keep a close watch on the others,' and he uttered a quick laugh, then looked grave. Devan's agitation returned and he knew that when he returned to his room it would fester all night. Mr. Bhairam added, 'I always win at the races, Swami,' and Devan began to wonder how he could reconcile the two statements. He would need a plan to get the stable-hands totally under his control; perhaps he should instruct them in Hinduism. Would Punam help him? Where was Punam now? Where were the others?

Mr. Bhairam merely looked around, and said they were somewhere: they were usually around; maybe it was because Athan had left and they weren't sure of what was happening.

Later that night, back in his room, listening to the sound of the horses, Devan felt an impulse to go back to the stables all alone, in the pitch blackness to talk to Destiny. Would the horse snort as before? But he soon fell asleep, tired from his mental and physical exertions.

Early the next morning, remembering his resolve, he headed for the stables. He found Punam, a thin-faced, long-limbed boy in his early twenties; he looked even younger, and Punam was eager to make his acquaintance. 'I hear plenty 'bout you, Swami,' he said.

'You have?'

'Yes. But you know anything 'bout training horses?'

Devan looked quizzically at him, then said yes. Hadn't he trained Gosai's filly?

'You hear 'bout the Syndicate, Swami?' Punam asked next.

'What's dat?'

'Mr. Bhairam na tell you 'bout it?' Punam looked puzzled.

Devan began to wonder what else he ought to know. He continued looking quizzically at Punam's thin features, not unlike his own son's he thought. Punam smiled awkwardly, and explained: 'That's why Jacob Athan lef', Swami. He gone to the Syndicate stables. You see, he want Mr. Bhairam to link up wid dem also, but Mr. Bhairam is sure Destiny go prove heself again at the October meeting.' Punam's eyes gleamed with satisfaction, and Devan pictured the horse and what he'd wanted to do in the pitch blackness. Punam continued, 'You see, Swami, de others don't tink Destiny stand a chance widout Jacob Athan – since he lef' I mean.'

'They tink dat, eh?'

'Yes – the Syndicate.'

'Who's they, eh?' Devan asked in what he hoped was an indifferent manner, though curiosity consumed him.

'Mr. Hassim is one of the founders. He is a rich Muslim; Mr. Bhairam rival from long time back. And then he got one Mr. Williams wid he – he too is a rival.'

'Christian an' Muslim, eh?' Devan said loudly, thinking Mr. Bhairam was a true Hindu in not joining with them. He looked at Punam as if he wanted confirmation of this fact, but the boy merely laughed a little and added:

'Some of the stable boys also tink Destiny go lose in October.'

'No!' cried Devan, as if in pain; and suddenly everything was confusing. How could the stable-hands think that? Weren't they loyal to Mr. Bhairam.

Punam, taken aback by the other's sharp response, wasn't sure what to say next and muttered mechanically, 'Destiny must win.' Devan quickly repeated this in his high-pitched manner and led the way to the champion horse's stable, with Punam nearly running to keep up with him. But when they were standing in front of the horse, Devan didn't know what to do next. He stood looking at Destiny whilst Punam fidgeted and looked around, hoping the other stable-hands weren't looking.

'Snort,' said Devan.

The horse stood still, then slowly started turning round, as Devan repeated his command. When the horse turned round once more, Punam, looking at Devan, asked: 'You tryin' voice-training Swami?'

'What?'

'Voice-training.'

'Yes-yes,' Devan flustered for a second, then continued looking at the horse.

Punam added, 'Destiny full a' spirit, too, Swami.' The boy was now amused by Devan as much as by the horse's antics, and he continued looking from one to the other.

'Spirit, eh?' Devan asked.

'Mr. Athan say so.' And Punam laughed, wondering what to say, then added, 'Destiny runs like a possessed animal too.'

'Oh?' Devan moved closer to the horse, peering at it, while a smile crept along Punam's mouth for he was enjoying the effect his words were having on the trainer. Devan now impulsively peeped at the horse between its rear legs and muttered what a magnificent animal it was; yes, really magnificent. 'Possessed, too, eh?' he repeated, his eyes brightening and he looked at Punam again as if he wanted him to reaffirm this, leaving Punam more intrigued than ever.

'Destiny has good legs, Swami. No need to worry,' Punam ventured as he saw Devan still peering at the horse's hindquarters.

'No need to worry, eh?' Devan was still preoccupied.

'It never got foot trouble.'

'No foot trouble too, eh?'

Punam nodded, looking at Devan's expression all the while, still not sure what to make of him. When Punam left to join the other stable-hands, Devan continued looking, peering, then moved to the other horses and inspected them, though without the same degree of interest. By now the stable boys were watching him; he seemed to be engaged in a sort of ritual, muttering the horses' names loudly to himself: 'Chaperon... Bounty Boy... Zephyr...' He stopped. 'No Hindu names?' he asked, and began thinking of names from Hindu scripture which he could suggest to Mr. Bhairam. But when one of the horses snorted, giving him a minor fright, he gave this up and returned to his own quarters, still thinking of Destiny.

He found Mr. Bhairam waiting for him, a solemn look on his face: he wanted to talk and Devan almost guessed what it was all about. 'Destiny, eh? I just been there, Bhai,' he began.

'It's about Mr. Hassim,' said Bhairam. 'He came to see me.'

'The Muslim? Founder of the Syndicate?' Devan blurted out, his hot breath slashing into Mr. Bhairam's face.

Stepping back quickly, Mr Bhairam said, 'Yes. He thinks I'll be sorry. I've come to tell you–'

'No need. He's a Muslim. Besides, Destiny is full of spirit, an' possessed too!'

Mr. Bhairam considered this gibberish seriously, frowned, and after a while, mumbled, 'I don't understand, Swami.'

'Destiny boun' to win, Mr. Bhairam,' Devan replied, smiling as he was wont to do on such occasions.

'I am pleased to hear you say that. Everything will be okay in your hands now, I believe. I am busy with League elections, of course,' said Mr. Bhairam, fidgeting slightly and looking at Devan with increased curiosity.

'Them are Muslim an' Christian, our enemies,' Devan hissed, and Mr. Bhairam – as if Devan had now uttered an anathema before him – hurried away, leaving Devan to recall the quarrels among the religions at Providence Village, oblivious of the fact that in Georgetown religions and races often mixed for practical reasons, though sometimes uneasily. And he looked out from the window for Punam, thinking of Destiny and then the Syndicate.

ELEVEN

The sports page of the newspaper spread out before him on the floor, Devan began scanning it for news – as Punam had told him Jacob Athan often did. A caption caught his attention: ***ATHAN JOINS SYNDICATE***; Devan read the words out slowly to himself, grinned, but when he began reading the article, his finger stepping across each word, the grin vanished from his face.

> Jacob Athan, well-known trainer of Mr. Bhairam of Vlissengen, has left to join the newly-formed Syndicate. This is a great loss to Mr. Bhairam's stables and it could affect his chances in the upcoming October meeting, the most important in the year. Rumour has it that Athan has been trying for weeks to get Mr. Bhairam to link up with the Syndicate, but that he has refused on religious grounds.
>
> Jacob Athan, as is well-known, is one of the leading trainers in British Guiana, and even throughout the Caribbean; he has been responsible for most of Mr. Bhairam's successes on the racetrack with his top horse, the remarkable Destiny. But whether Destiny can repeat its performance in October against the Syndicate's imports from the Caribbean and elsewhere remains to be seen.

Devan paused to catch his breath; already he didn't like the tone of the article; the reporter was an enemy, and, his fingers once more following the words, he shook his head as he read on:

> It is learnt that Mr. Bhairam has chosen a virtual unknown in the racing world – one Swami Devan, a religious leader, a fanatic, – to replace Jacob Athan. This news has surprised everyone, including some of Mr. Bhairam's well- known Hindu friends in the All India League; it is even said that some of his stable-boys are affected by the move and that morale is low among them.
>
> How much is known of Swami Devan's horse-racing prowess is open to much doubt; it is believed he came from the Corentyne where horse-racing at Port Mourant has taken place, though of a much lower calibre that in Georgetown. Some people are beginning to say that Mr. Bhairam, who is seeking the important post of president of the All India League, is allowing religious sentiment to govern his horse-racing judgement. One source even has it that the swami has cast a spell on Mr. Bhairam! It is a known fact that the swami is increasingly getting close to Mr. Bhairam, and to Mrs. Bhairam as well. Maybe he will use wizardry as part of his training technique – as the stable boys are saying. Let us wait and see – in October!

Devan cast the paper aside in a fit, and fuming, he shouted, 'I go show them! I go show them. Wizardry indeed, eh?' He almost choked on his words as he circled his room quickly two or three times; then, as if not knowing what else to do, he hurried up the stairs to the main floor, passing Mrs. Bhairam on the way and ignoring her totally – she turning around in alarm and following him – to burst into Mr. Bhairam's private room. Breathing hard, Devan blurted out to his benefactor, 'See dis – the newspapers! See what they're sayin' now?' He stammered, almost apoplectic, his eyes widening.

Mr. Bhairam was in a calm mood, since he had just been meditating, and was very surprised to see Devan so agitated.

Mrs. Bhairam put her hand to her mouth as she looked at Devan's distraught expression, seeming as if she was about to become ill. Mr. Bhairam muttered calmly:

'What does it say, Swami?'

'Evil things: The reporter is an enemy! Who tell he to print such things is also enemy!'

Mr. Bhairam leant forward in a slow, deliberate manner and, as if he had all the time in the world, scanned the article. Devan, expecting him to burst out in rage, found it almost impossible to contain himself, especially when Mr. Bhairam said inanely, 'So you've been reading the newspapers, eh?' 'Athan must have given the reporter this news.'

'No, Swami.'

'Who then?'

Mr. Bhairam leant back like a man who had swallowed food which wasn't to his liking and the discomfort was causing him great pain; whilst Mrs. Bhairam still had her resolute air of wonderment.

Mr. Bhairam's face appeared contorted and Devan thought he still wasn't seeing correctly: that he was really imagining it all.

'I did,' Mr. Bhairam said.

'You did?'

Mr. Bhairam's face relaxed, and he smiled widely because he felt he had taken care of Devan's agitation, and he added, 'You must take it easy, Swami. You see I told them you have become my trainer; indeed I have.' He laughed a little jocularly, 'And you see, whatever they write will not affect my chances at all, a horse doesn't read, does it?' Devan reflected on this. Mr. Bhairam continued, 'For now, I must concentrate on the All India League, you see; I hope you understand, eh?' He looked penetratingly at Devan.

Devan figured he'd had a sudden insight into Mr. Bhairam's mind, and he smiled uneasily, feeling that he was now beginning to understand his benefactor better. Destiny *was* bound to win. Let them write what they wanted; let the Syndicate or Athan, or whoever else, spread false lies; and he murmured, 'Of course, I should know; I should indeed, Mr. Bhairam.' He patted the sides of his vaselined head, thinking that Mr Bhairam had indeed shown acumen. He saw too, for the first time his direct benefit to Mr. Bhairam, for in appointing him, a stalwart Hindu – one well-known on the East Coast – Mr. Bhairam was trying to assure his supporters in the League that he was a Hindu all the way, since his trainer was now a Hindu. Quietly he dropped the newspapers, as Mr. Bhairam, added:

'You mustn't read the newspapers, Swamiji. They never print exactly what you tell them.'

Devan nodded heavily as if he now had an insight into the workings of the newspaper trade, and he walked back to his room with a doleful air. There, not knowing what else to do, he scanned the rest of the newspapers for news about himself or the League, or anything else that meant something to him. When he couldn't find anything, he picked up the *Gita* and read loudly, believing that whatever evil was present in the room because of the newspaper article would now be exorcised. Satisfied, he closed his eyes and meditated, and a serene, almost blissful state came to him, his thoughts wandering, drifting: in this state he imagined himself teaching the stable-boys about Hinduism. He smiled as this thought took firmer grip on his mind; now there would be no interference from a Board of Governors, none whatsoever; and he imagined the boys becoming pious, well-versed in Hindu ethics. Each every moment they talked to each other it would be with sweetness, and they would be uttering sayings from the scriptures and their thoughts would only be on virtue, holiness, and goodness; and they would sit together, three or four of them at a time, in the stables, and with legs folded in the traditional manner they would hum mantras, no matter how loudly the horses neighed round about them. Such would be their transformation, all because of his teaching!

And he figured nothing would please Mr. Bhairam more; word would get around that Mr. Bhairam's stable boys were a new breed of Hindu youth: they would form the core of an army of Hindu workers which would spread across Guiana. Even Muslim and Christian youths would become converts to Hinduism; and all would be working on behalf of Mr. Bhairam in his struggle against the lawyer Sarwan Singh. He saw Punam as the staunchest of these young Hindus, he would have daily consultations with him: together they would plan strategy after strategy; Punam would report to him on the progress of the 'army'; his own son Jotish might be one of the young leaders, maybe even taking over the Berbice battalion when the time was ripe.

He got up and walked about his room, whistling as the idea appealed to him more and more. A knock on his door, and he opened it, beaming. Mr. Bhairam stood before him, amazed to see this transformation of Devan's mood, but he managed to say:

'I am going to Enmore tomorrow, Swamiji, to open a new school there. How would you like to come with me? Maybe you will... well, you may be called upon to make a speech.' Mr. Bhairam laughed nervously as he stood before the beaming face.

Devan beamed even more, as nostalgia for the East Coast flooded into him. 'Yes, indeed, I love to, I want to!'

Mr. Bhairam, the frown of a deep thought hovering on his face, added: 'The elections, you know, Swamiji – it's only a month away.'

'Indeed, the elections. I go talk about Hindu ethics, eh?' He continued to beam, to sparkle, the stable boys in his mind, an entire army.

'Oh?'

'Yes-yes!'

'And maybe about voting matters too, eh, Swami,' cautioned the other, like a man lost, and he started hurrying back to his private room, even as Devan hollered after him:

'That too!'

On the East Coast highway Mr. Bhairam, driving along

in an extremely pleasant mood, talked about his various plans for the League, garrulous in a way Devan hadn't previously seen; but by now there were few things about his benefactor which surprised Devan – even Mr. Bhairam's heavy frowns, which Devan ascribed merely to an instinctive habit, like an irrepressible yawn. Indeed, they accepted each other now, and Devan surmised that in this respect Mrs. Bhairam had helped him enormously; no doubt she talked to her husband about him, explaining his habits as stemming from his destiny in life, no less.

He looked at Mr. Bhairam who was talking about his dream to establish preparatories in every district in Guiana, though after a while Devan no longer listened. *He* dwelt on teaching the stable-boys Hindu ethics, though he didn't mention this to Mr. Bhairam; he hoped to surprise him before long – Mr. Bhairam would see for himself how pious his workers had become.

And then Mr. Bhairam, looking ahead carefully as he drove, his stomach touching the steering wheel from time to time because of his awkward stance, casually mentioned that the Georgetown Preparatory now had one hundred and twenty pupils.

'One hundred and twenty?' Devan asked in disbelief, thinking of the pandemonium that number of children would create; he imagined a suave Aurobindo Ghose losing his composure and using his whip as the children bawled out obscenities to him, some no doubt fleeing. He smiled. 'How de teacher doing?' he asked, a gloating feeling getting the better of him.

'He has four assistants.'

'Four assistants?' Devan thought he hadn't heard correctly.

'Yes. The Board thought it fit he should have as many. Aurobindo is really the principal you know.'

Envy gripped Devan; it seared him. Neither said anything for a minute, and the houses whipped past on both sides as the Mercedes sped along, Mr. Bhairam focusing steadfastly ahead, his stomach twitching as from time to time it collided with the steering wheel when he had to make a sharp turn to avoid hitting a donkey crossing the road. But the entire scene was a blur to Devan; he was still thinking about the school, about the principal Aurobindo Ghose, about the parents coming to visit and making a fuss.

'He's getting a salary of five hundred dollars a month,' Mr. Bhairam added absent-mindedly. Devan was aghast and he cried, 'Favouritism! I was only getting fifty!' The force of this response seemed to cause the steering wheel to jerk at an angle, and Mr. Bhairam's stomach correspondingly twitched, and he frowned, muttering, 'Ah, Swami, Aurobindo is a Bachelor of Arts, a Sanskrit scholar.'

'Bachelor of Arts, eh?' Devan growled quietly, still in a daze as he looked ahead at the winding road, at the cow now ambling across it, with Mr. Bhairam getting ready to swerve and then simultaneously pressing on the brake and causing the tyres to screech loudly as the cow suddenly jumped forward, hopping, then careering across to the other side of the road. All of this made Devan's heart throb violently, since it wasn't often he was in a car to experience such hazards.

'He's been made an honorary member of the League,' Mr. Bhairam murmured.

'Everyone respects him very much; the parents have been saying what a wonderful teacher he is, and Sarwan Singh, my rival, is very pleased.' The tone was without resentment; only a half-rueful expression shadowed Mr. Bhairam's face. But Devan took no notice of this, for, still dazed, he was looking out for another cow on the road, bracing himself for another sudden swerve, his entire body rigid. Mr. Bhairam continued, 'There's even talk of putting Aurobindo to run for treasurer in the coming elections.'

Devan, nonplussed, concentrated on the animals by the road; they seemed to be everywhere now: cows, horses, sheep, goats, a donkey here and there, each ready to dash across the road in front of the Mercedes. He imagined them all lined up ahead on the road, against the shimmer of the asphalt and Mr.

Bhairam, his stomach twitching convulsively, about to step on the brakes with all his might. Instinctively Devan stretched out a hand to the dashboard, his muscles rigid, and he closed his eyes and muttered a prayer, hoping that this wasn't to be the end of his life. Mr. Bhairam indeed pressed on the brake, but the Mercedes came to a quiet stop. 'We have arrived, Swami,' the executive said, and Devan opened his eyes to see a large crowd of people standing on both sides of the road and Mr. Bhairam smiling expansively at the greeting he was being accorded by the Enmore community.

There was nothing like a crowd to make Devan feel good again, and rubbing his eyes as if he wanted imaginary scales to fall, he rushed out beside Mr. Bhairam to shake hands. And he saw a familiar face coming forward – Pandit Gocolram – even though Mahaica was about twenty-five miles from Enmore. While the Enmore officials busied themselves and fussed round Mr. Bhairam, Devan and Gocolram exchanged greetings like old pals.

'Mekking any progress, Swami?' asked Gocolram casually, looking resplendent in a white dhoti, his face a healthy brown in the sunshine.

'I not a member of the League yet, you know, if tha's what you mean, Panditiji.'

Their tone was continually cordial, and Gocolram, secretly happy that Devan's favours with Mr. Bhairam hadn't increased, replied: 'Your time come, once Mr. Bhairam is president.'

Devan looked at the pandit, heartened by this encouragement, and he was even more convinced that Gocolram was still his best friend. He muttered, 'Training haas is difficult work, Panditji.' He was about to tell him about his plan to teach the stable-boys Hindu ethics, but instead said, 'Destiny boun' to win.'

Gocolram replied, 'You mus' watch out for the Syndicate though, Swami. It go cause trouble for Bhai; me been hear rumours that Sarwan Singh is thinkin' of joining wid the Syndicate now.'

Devan was aghast. He looked around to see the Enmore Hindus still making a fuss over Mr. Bhairam, who was smiling all the time he was shaking hands, almost twenty at once it seemed to Devan.

'Impossible! A prominent Hindu join wid Christians and Muslims! No!' It was too much for Devan, and he let out a muffled cry, surprised at Gocolram's knowledge of this information and even more astonished when the pandit, whom he expected to express consternation and condemnation, said with a stoically unperturbed air, 'Ah, Swamiji, all men are brothers.'

Gocolram took careful note of the worried look on Devan's face and felt good. But when Devan in desperation asked him what he thought of Mr. Bhairam's chances in the coming elections, Gocolram smiled beguilingly: 'Have no fear, Swami. The rural Hindus are all behind Bhai. Me come here to find out the extent of their support.' And he smiled again genially as Devan looked ever more worried.

TWELVE

'O Ommipotent! O Omniscient!' began the officiating pandit, and the Enmore devotees in the temple responded with appropriate *ohms*. Sitting in front on the dais, as always close to Mr. Bhairam, Devan muttered under his breath, 'O Creator of the Universe,' and inhaled the aroma of the women's talc and perfumes and for a second lost his concentration. When the officiating pandit concluded his invocation, Devan still had his eyes closed but Gocolram, alongside him, nudged him gently and Devan opened his eyes at once, his line of vision falling on a group of women in the middle of the gathering – particularly on a half-veiled woman who didn't look unlike Tara. Devan kept his attention riveted to her; she looked exactly the way Tara looked on her wedding day, and he sighed. Gocolram, looking sideways at him, whispered: 'What's the matter, Swamiji?' Mr. Bhairam, glanced at him too, while Devan deliberately lowered his head so he wouldn't see more of the half-veiled girl, hard as this was to do. Was it her? He looked up again, more curious and anxious than ever, and his eyes roved round the gathering for his son Jotish: the boy had to be somewhere. Again Gocolram and Bhairam glanced at him, and when Devan closed his eyes and muttered a quick prayer, Gocolram looked askance at what he thought was Devan's excessive religious zeal.

When Devan opened his eyes, deliberately looking away from the cluster of women, he listened to the officiating priest whining sycophantically, 'All praise must be given to Mr. Bhairam, brothers and sisters. All praise indeed, and for him to come amongst us when he is so busy with plans to become president of All India League.'

A ripple of smiles broke from the crowd and half a dozen or so applauded. Devan, unable to suppress his nervous excitement, tittered and instinctively leant over to Gocolram muttering, 'Boun' to win.' The latter responded serenely, 'Ah, yes,' tapping Devan lightly on the leg as if he was acknowledging a child.

Next the officiating priest read out the names of those who had contributed handsomely towards the building of the Enmore school, and as was to be expected, Mr. Bhairam's was prominent, his contribution being the largest; again appropriate ripples of applause followed. Devan looked up at the ceiling, trying his best not to look either at the half-veiled girl or at the youths at the back who reminded him of his persecutors in Providence village. He was surprised out of this momentary absorption when the officiating pandit cried out in his sing-song voice, as if he was the bearer of unexpected tidings:

'We're happy to have among us none other than Swami Devan. Swamiji, I know, is no stranger to some of you; some of we hear him in Mahaica an' in other places on the East Coast and we know too dat he is famous in Berbice and in Corentyne in particular. He is a fine orator, there's no doubt.' He grinned, and as if in anticipation of entertainment to come, a ripple rose from the crowd. Mr. Bhairam himself smiled, which caused further agreeable ripples, whilst Gocolram lifted his head up like a stork's and surveyed the audience, especially the boys at the back, as if to say to them that this was what they were waiting for. Devan inhaled more perfume and felt tremulous. The officiating pandit continued:

'Bhais and baheens, Swami Devan is highly esteemed among us. We must not forget that is because of Mr. Bhairam's esteem for him that he mek him the first teacher of the Georgetown Prepar'tory – the same one we hear so much about. It a great shame though that the Board of Gov'nors Mr. Sarwan Singh is head of decide to replace he widout knowing Mr. Bhairam's feelings on the matter.'

Devan touched the side of his head as he thought of Aurobindo Ghose. 'Bachelor of Arts,' he muttered disconsolately and Gocolram – always with a keen but discreet ear for Devan's unexpected utterances – added with a smile, 'Four assistants also.' Devan looked at the Mahaica pandit and wasn't sure about the expression on his face. The officiating pandit was still speaking: 'As you all know, our beloved Mr. Bhairam don't like public speaking, being a man of action.' Brief applause followed in acknowledgement of Mr. Bhairam's shortcomings, as the Enmore pandit added, 'That's why we are able to have this school here today. Now, it is with great pleasure that I call 'pon Swamiji to address you. *Acha*, Swamiji!'

Getting up, making a mental note not to look at the half-veiled girl, Devan tried to look beyond the audience, beyond the youths at the back. He felt determined, inspired, and he began talking about the importance of a solid Hindu education, waving his short hands about and chopping the air all around him, spittle flying out of his mouth like sparks. There was nothing like an audience to make him feel this way. He scattered his remarks with quotations from the *Upanishads* and the *Ramayana* almost in the same breath; he referred to the *Mahabharata* as if it told of recent events which had taken place in Guiana, and he talked of Arjuna, Krishna, Rama and Sita as if they were highly respected members of the All India League and of his benefactor as if he was one of that company of deities. 'Bhais and baheens in our great religion, the Hindu temple and the new school must always remind we of Mr. Bhairam's great generosity and benevolence, for he a blessed man, one of we own – we must all remember dat. Yes, our divine Mr. Bhairam not easily corrupt like some others who shall be nameless, who go mix up our religion wid Christians and Muslims, for dem two religions, mark my words, are of de same root, de same story of Abraham and Moses taken from de Ole Testament. But not Hinduism. Our religion has endured throughout the centuries, longer dan any other; it is the way of life that keep we motherland of India still a blessed country. It is from that same country that we ancestors came, that we own Mr. Bhairam's father from...' Here he paused, eager to mention his own father, but was prevented from doing this when someone coughed in the audience, and he was about to look at the half-veiled girl, but just remembered to lift his head and look straight ahead: 'Mark my words,' he continued, 'in dis same Guiana we Hindus de majority, and bhais and baheens, we still de children of India, she sons and daughters; remember dis well; we go build such a school here dat go make sure we Hindu heritage is preserve through teaching our young people wherever they are. An' schools go be built in other parts of Guiana too beside, in the county of Berbice, as far as Providence Village, and all along de East and West Coast of Demerara, and in Wakenaam in de county of Essequibo, thoughout de length an' breadth of this country; even in places like stables or in business office in the capital we go make sure Hindus are always a proud an' blessed people.' (LOUD APPLAUSE)

Devan wiped beads of perspiration from his face and he added, 'Yes, brothers and sisters, we mus'n forget Mr. Bhairam on election day, for when Mr. Bhairam turn president of de All India League he go build all dese schools – dese prepar'tories – everywhere, in every rural district so that we sacred religion always go be on top an' Guiana go be a land for Hindus, always!' (FURTHER APPLAUSE)

Devan continued for another fifteen minutes, quoting liberally from the *Gita*, the *Ramayana*, and then from *Mundkopanishad* as he tried to give breadth to his words and he intoned in the sweetest manner he was capable of: 'Of de gods Brahmaji, de creator an' protector of de universe, was self-born firs'. He give out knowledge a' reality to he eldest child Athvara and dat knowledge deal with brahman, de eternal pure consciousness, knowledge of all knowledge an' foundation of all sciences.' For a while Devan wasn't sure what he was saying, but murmurs of approval came to his ears, especially from the older Hindus, and encouraged to go on, he found himself quoting from Rudyard Kipling as he'd done in Providence Village the words pouring out as he gesticulated and believed that he was the Tarlogie pandit all over again – even though an independent observer might have remarked on his resemblance to one of the hot gospellers who now and again came to the rural districts to preach the Christian gospel. Devan now cried out against corruption and evil, 'for all Hindus to refrain from alcohol, smoking and other forms of evil-doing; to be celibate and try to live sanctified lives, meditate night an' day an' think upon goodness an' truth. Let the spiritual life always be you goal.' For a while Devan imagined himself addressing the stable-boys; it stopped him thinking about the half-veiled girl, but then, in a flash, he imagined her getting up and screaming at him, 'Why yuh na work like everybody else and mine de children, eh?' This was enough to unsettle him, and in a lower, though steady tone, he sighed and reluctantly concluded.

'Bhais and baheens, always strive to be in harmony wid the Omnipotent, Omniscient God of the Universe!' He mumbled a few more words, a little unsurely now, then walked back to his seat, his head whirling with the excitement of his delivery even though for a moment he wasn't sure if he was still a believer in Hinduism or what he believed, but it was God nevertheless, he told himself. Mr. Bhairam leaned across to him and said, 'Brilliant speech, Swamiji,' as if he was a new convert to Hinduism. 'Very inspiring.' Gocolram also leaned forward and muttered congratulation, even though Devan didn't catch the words very plainly. His mind was still whirling, and he looked about him and saw Hindus coming forward to express felicitations to Mr. Bhairam, but only a few to actually congratulate him. He looked uncomfortably disappointed and Gocolram, laughing a little, said, 'Never mind, Swami, you is now a race-horse trainer, eh? Destiny is on yuh side, eh.' Devan didn't reply, but stretched out a tentacle of a hand to an elderly Hindu congratulating him. Gocolram, standing back, still smiling genially, then added, 'Another t'ing, Swami, you must rememba dat only financial members are allowed to vote in League elections. Georgetown members, you know, are very wealthy.'

Devan looked at the next work-worn hand stretched out to him and he felt pained; he glanced at Mr. Bhairam who was laughing loudly now and shaking hands as if this was all he wanted to do for the rest of his life. Devan looked away, dismayed – and just then he saw the half-veiled girl close by in a knot of women; he was convinced now that she was Tara. He cried out, softly at first, 'Tara, Tara!' But another set of hands jutted out before him and dark and brown faces smiled all round him. Devan, pushing them aside, hurried to the exit. 'Tara!' Tara!' he called out at the top of his voice. But she was gone, and Gocolram, once more close by and unfailingly serene, said at his shoulder, 'Ah, Swamiji, you mustn' give up hope, eh.' Devan looked at him with an expression of uncertainty, feeling his loss, deeper even than he'd felt when he left Providence Village, as he recalled the faces of his wife and children. Gocolram led him back to the Mercedes, where Mr. Bhairam, still surrounded by more Hindus, waited for them.

Devan was now only too eager to be away, but not before casting another hopeful look amongst the knots of women for Tara, and then for his son, Jotish, amongst the groups of boys walking idly about.

The Mercedes sped along the East Coast road on the way back to Georgetown, Mr. Bhairam's stomach once more braced against the steering wheel. He was relaxed and expansive. 'I have lots of plans ahead, many plans, Swami, once I become president of the All India League. You see, I will indeed build schools all across the coastland of our beloved Guiana. We will have another India right here, India an' Africa maybe, each able to live side by side.' Mr. Bhairam's eyes shone as he looked straight ahead, and Devan nodded in some confusion as he remembered Gocolram's words. But he allowed himself to imagine being the administrator of all these schools, even replacing Sarwan Singh on the Board of Governors; maybe then he would give direct instructions to Aurobindo Ghose on how to teach. He smiled.

The Mercedes jolted forward as Mr. Bhairam braked to

avoid hitting a dog; the gleam momentarily seemed to disappear from his eyes, and he said quietly, 'I wish my sons were here to help me in all the work, Swamiji.'

'Your sons? Where are they?'

'Oh, my boys are in England, studying, you know. One will become a doctor and the other will be an engineer. My daughter, my beloved Indrani, she's in America studying to be a beauty technician. I hope they all marry abroad, Swamiji.'

He turned and looked at Devan, the latter in a greater whirl than ever, wondering if Mr. Bhairam's children were devoted Hindus; but he didn't ask, fearing what the answer might be. And closing his eyes, he allowed his thoughts to dwell on an image of his son Jotish, dressed in jacket and tie like Mr. Bhairam's sons no doubt, and sailing in a ship... for England! And he was in a total blur now, as if past and present were all one, and the future itself was part of the overwhelming blur taking over his life; in this instant too, destiny no longer seemed to matter; nothing really mattered. And waves lashed against the sides of the ship, which rocked and seemed to bend perilously low; and Jotish was still in that ship; and maybe... yes maybe, the ship was heading – not for England – but India... It was still a blur; he felt painfully disoriented and longed desperately to get out of it.

THIRTEEN

In the stables Punam gave careful thought to the idea of becoming a zealous Hindu. He felt Devan was sometimes strange, his behaviour odd, but he didn't mind that too much. And he figured that if all the stable boys and youths everywhere became staunch Hindus, British Guiana would be a place without strife and turmoil; the politicians might even quarrel less among themselves; maybe everyone would vote alike. No doubt Swami Devan could promote the idea of a special Hindu sect, an elite corps, one associated with Mr. Bhairam's name: Mr. Bhairam's Hindu soldiers marching for Hinduism! This could be New World Hinduism, which Swami Devan had talked about before. And many youths from across the Caribbean, the rest of South America, and those in Canada and the United States could soon be part of the movement. And before long, the New World might have more zealous Hindus than India itself! He smiled, the idea was full of possibilities; it gripped his mind intensely.

He imagined slogans for coping with difficulties closer to home. 'Save Guiana through Hinduism' and, 'Young Hinduism on the Rise'; and yet another, 'Save Guiana from Communism through Hindu Holiness!' He beamed at his inventiveness. But his enthusiasm diminished as he thought of the coming race and the Swami's habit of looking at the horses in their stables late at night, so unlike Mr. Athan's careful preparation.

The other boys, playing cards and slapping dominoes, hailed him as he walked past the stables, deep in thought. Punam wondered how Swami Devan would get them interested in the horses again and ready to do their work.

They'd become slack since Athan left. He found himself drifting towards Devan's quarters and tapped against the window. Though Devan was about to start meditating, he was pleased to see Punam; he was getting bored with being alone. When he saw Punam glancing at his books, Devan was only too willing to show him the heavy volumes one by one, and added, 'Maybe me too go write a book one day.'

'About horses, Swami?' asked Punam innocently.

'No, no. About us.'

'Us?'

'Yes – we Hindus. We na belong here. White people only bring we here fo' cut sugar-cane and wuk in rice field. We belong to India,' he added, 'that is our real home. We na come here to slave like African people. Slavery done now.'

Punam looked at him, impressed by his manner and feeling a new-found pride in himself as an Indian. 'Maybe you could write about New World Hinduism, Swami.' Punam was more intrigued than ever when Devan added, 'There's money in exposin' white people injustice to our parents, Punam.'

'Money?' Punam sat down, looking at the framed pictures on the wall depicting various deities with many arms and legs, some with halcyon expressions in idyllic surroundings, much in contrast to Devan's room into which no cleaner was allowed. Punam concentrated on one illustration depicting the trinity Brahma-Vishnu-Mahesh, which he'd seen before.

'Yes, white people promise we compensation for coming to Guiana an' they not pay up yet,' added Devan, also glancing at the picture, though his mind was on more immediate history.

Punam nodded reflectively, thinking of the sugar estates he'd seen – he often wondered why fate had led him away from working on a sugar estate to being a stable-boy in Georgetown. Devan added, 'They owe we thousands of pounds!'

'Thousands of pounds, eh?' Punam for a moment allowed his mind to dwell on the fact that the stable-boys were poorly paid; maybe, eventually, Mr. Bhairam would really start paying better. Punam glanced at the picture once more, then slowly told Devan the thoughts he'd been having about Hinduism. Devan smiled. Punam was showing promise, he had vision.

'You ever tink of becoming a pandit?' he asked.

Punam reflected for a while, thinking of an uncle who was a pandit but who was also rumoured to be an alcoholic, of the tiresome rituals and the unsatisfactory discipline which a pandit's life involved. Not wanting to go through such ordeals himself, he quickly said, 'I prefer working wid horses, Swami.' He looked at Devan, and the latter not knowing what else to say, began talking about his own love for horses. He recalled the two horses in Mahaica when he'd sat under the mango tree and how he'd enjoyed watching them astride each other; then Gosai's filly came back to him too. All the while Punam looked closely at him and felt he was getting to know him better. Much better.

Next Devan started talking about Jotish and how he hoped one day his son would become a pandit. 'Jotish used to gather hibiscus flowers for me every morning an' he use to sit down wid me and meditate.'

'Oh?' replied Punam, noting a sorrowful wistfulness on Devan's face, as he continued.

'Now, you see, my Jotish gone wid he modder an' he turn out a rascal.' The forlorn air with which he said this touched Punam immensely.

'Maybe Jotish is not a rascal, Swamiji.'

'You really tink so, eh?' Devan brightened.

'Yes. Maybe you go see him before long.' Punam smiled.

'See he, eh?' asked Devan, at once thinking of the half-veiled girl at Enmore; and he grew suddenly afraid, and Punam wasn't sure what was the matter with him, because his hands started trembling and his eyes swirled vacantly. Punam got up quickly and left, thinking he didn't really understand the trainer at all.

The stable-boys, watching Punam come from the Villa, stopped playing cards, and came up to him. Amid snickers they wanted to know what he and Swami Devan discussed; they had seen them together; they knew too that Punam's uncle was a pandit and that he wasn't like the rest of them; and they had often chaffed him for his devotion to his work with the horses.

'What Swami do in his room, Punam?' they asked.

Sensing their readiness to ridicule, Punam said: 'He reads heavy volumes,' and he hesitated, not wanting to say more, though he was usually compliant.

'What else, Punam? Tell we!'

'He meditates... night an' day.'

'Oh?' they laughed and sneered loudly and came round him, eager to hear more, ready to gossip.

Punam, his thin lips throbbing, answered: 'True-true. He a strict Hindu-man you know. He not like the rest of you! Devan go achieve perfec' bliss.' This phrase immediately caused further derisive laughter, and Punam grew hot at the tips of his ears. Boysie, the oldest of the boys, advanced closer and said, 'Dat swami is a fake!'

'He isn't! I seen him reading heavy volumes wid me own eyes. Besides, he a fine orator.'

'Who tell you dat?' they pressed, wanting to know more, to laugh again.

Punam blurted out, 'Me uncle – he a pandit; he know. He hear Swami Devan on the East Coast; he hear him wid he own ears! Hundreds of others hear he too.'

The boys leant forward, shaking their ears at him, jeering. Punam felt it was no use trying to convince them, much less to tell them about New World Hinduism, which he'd been hoping to do when the time was ripe. He sighed and cast a glance towards the Villa. Govind, the youngest of the boys, sneered: 'So dat is why you so close to Swami, eh? I bet he na tell you how to groom Destiny?'

Punam looked from one to an other, remaining frozen for a while, confused. He wished they would begin to believe in Swami Devan as he did. Anand challenged next. 'How come you always laugh at you uncle – and now you believe in Swami

Devan?'

'Cause... cause...' Punam was embarrassed, unsure. 'Look I not ashamed of he. Nothing wrong wid being a pandit! Dat's what Swami Devan say – too many young people ashame of dey religion. Is because we so far away from India. Yes, and too many of we become Christians an' atheists! But things change round here. Mr. Bhairam going build Hindu schools all over and everybody believe in Hinduism before long. Even Africans go believe!' This caused further laughter. But, undeterred, Punam added, 'Yes, even white people go start believing in Hinduism; you go see. They go start goin' to India, true-true. An' some go start comin' here too, fo' meet wid we own Swami Devan. Yes, is true!'

Punam was on the verge of tears, and the boys watched him with a mixture of pleasure and alarm, because they'd never seen him become so emotional before. And in this distress, Punam's vision of New World Hinduism fled; and when a horse neighed he quickly went towards Destiny's stable, concentrating only on the horse, hoping it would win once more: this would be the vindication over the boys.

Meanwhile, in his room, Devan was giving more thought to his idea of teaching the stable-boys. He saw the boys forming a community close to the Villa and having regular pujas on Sundays and singing *bhajans*, the *dhyanam* and *avahavan*, invocations to Vishnu, Ganesh, Kartikeya, Lakshmi, Durga devi and many others, with recitations of *stotras* and *namavali*. He felt like weeping with joy as the vision gripped him; and he saw Punam assisting him, and Jotish as well, for his son would be close by, always.

All that afternoon he thought about this community of souls so close to the Villa, so close to the horses; the idea so consumed him that he could hardly sleep that night.

Early the next morning, his hands trembling, he clapped loudly in readiness to begin his pedagogic task. He looked around, but no one appeared. He called out loudly, but only Punam arrived, to see Devan, hands akimbo, in the middle of the compound. 'Is anything the matter, Swamiji?' he asked.

Devan stuttered for a few seconds. 'Ethics!' he blurted out. 'Hindu ethics!'

In a moment of silence they looked at each other. A horse neighed, the smell of oats in the air. 'Ethics, eh?' Punam asked mechanically. He kept looking at Swami Devan and right then he wished Jacob Athan hadn't left.

The boys started coming in – one by one. They seemed to know that Devan had some scheme in mind, and they waited for him, sneers written across their faces. Devan fidgeted, but when he spoke it was vehemently: 'You all goin' learn Hindu ethics. All ah you! They stared at him in confusion: how dramatic and ridiculous he was, the words rushing out. 'Tell me what you know about Hindu culture, eh? Tell me dat – all ah you. I mus' know.'

But they laughed, the essence of what Devan was trying to do coming home to them. They looked at Punam and laughed even more. And Devan cried out, 'Stop it! Stop it, you fools! You na see me tryin' to teach you Hindu ethics an' culture!'

The boys looked at one another as Devan cried, 'The stables going to be a place of God and holiness! You hear me? The whole worl' mus' know about Mr. Bhairam's stables and about holiness. Remember, he go be president of the All India League an' his stables mus' be like no other in Guiana; it musn't be like Christian an' Mussulman stable, eh?' He ranted and raved about the Syndicate; and the boys continued to look at one another in amazement, and one sniggered. Devan, unable to control his temper at this insolence, lashed out:

'From now on you mus' paint all the stables white! There mus' be no dirt; make everything clean an' bright. Only this way we go drive out de devil!'

'Wha' devil, Swami?' asked Boysie. The others took this up like a refrain.

'Eh-eh, wha' devil this, Swami?'

Punam, a little distance away, lowered his head, embarrassed. He looked at Devan again to see him stammering, confused by the others' increasing insolence as he blurted out, 'The Syndicate, dammit!' Punam shuddered and watched the boys laughing openly. 'Is Hindu culture goin' to defeat the Syndicate, Swami?' asked Govind with mock-seriousness.

'Yes-yes. It will!'

Another quickly asked, 'Is true culture comes from agriculture?'

This added to Devan's wrath as he recalled the youngsters at Providence Village, and spittle bubbled at the corners of his mouth as he snapped, 'No, you mustn' tink dat! No! You ignorant – all o' you!'

But this shriek didn't intimidate the boys who only continued sniggering and laughing, and another asked, 'How can Hindu culture help us train haas, eh?'

Devan's zeal to transform their lives and make them into staunch Hindus suddenly vanished. Punam watched the dismay spread across his face and felt pity for him. But Devan, seeming to recover his resilience, murmured very audibly, 'Work is sacred.'

'Who say dat, Swami?'

'Gandhi,' Devan replied, not looking directly at any of them, not even at Punam.

'Did Gandhi know how to train haas? Or he know only about cow?'

Devan dug his heels into the ground and the others made more sneering sounds. Devan at once lifted his head and cried out in pain, 'You illiterate! All ah you – I know fron the beginning! Gandhi a great man; he get purity of soul...' He didn't know what else to say, and as he fought to regain his composure, another asked, 'What about the Syndicate, Swami?'

'It must not win!' Devan let out in a short gasp. Punam was about to stretch out an arm to him in a consoling way, but Devan was already hurrying back to his quarters as if he was indeed escaping from the devil, the boys' laughter pursuing him through the compound.

Devan bolted his door and closed the windows firmly.

Thinking Yoga exercises might help, he attempted a headstand and fought to stay upright, the blood rushing to his neck and head. He felt his veins knot, yet he resolutely kept his hold and held his breath, his eyes almost bursting from their sockets. It was then that Mr. Bhairam knocked on his door. Upside down, Devan called out, 'Who dat?'

When he heard Mr. Bhairam's voice he quickly got back to an upright position, his eyes and face blood-red; he opened the door and glared at a very surprised Mr. Bhairam. 'Good news or bad news?' Devan asked with a gasp.

Mr. Bhairam, thinking Devan had suddenly contracted a strange disease, frowned so that ropes of flesh bulged on his forehead, answered, 'Bad news.'

'I knew it!'

'You did?'

'Yes – because of the boys. Dem is all rascals!'

'What boys?'

'The stable-hands,' pointed Devan, military-like through the window, having difficulty controlling his agitation. 'They have the devil wid dem!'

Mr. Bhairam felt his face become stiff. 'I come to tell you that Sarwan Singh has joined the Syndicate.'

'He is an opportunist!'

Mr. Bhairam, knitting his eyebrows in a vague, involuntary way, replied calmly: 'Human nature, Swamiji.' He frowned again. 'It's the elections I'm most worried about. Destiny, naturally, will take care of the Syndicate.'

'Elections, eh?'

'Yes. The rural Hindus will never vote for the lawyer, of course, now that he has formally linked up with Muslims and Christians.' He smiled, though a little uncomfortably.

'You right – they'll never vote for he!' Devan answered, and he started laughing now, uncontrollably, as Mr. Bhairam looked at him in dull amazement. When the latter hurried back to the upper storey, he too began laughing. Mrs. Bhairam thought Swami Devan was indeed having a strange effect on her husband.

FOURTEEN

Signs everywhere exhorted Hindus to vote: on old barrels, dilapidated shacks, outhouses, cow-pens, on culverts in the city; the signs urged everyone to vote for Mr. Bhairam as a philanthropist, a man of vision. In business places in the city other signs, more discreetly, characterised Sarwan Singh as a sell-out to Christians and Moslems. Ganesh Lall, of course, was chiefly responsible for getting these signs put up as he tried to counter the lawyer's mounting popularity. Lall, indeed, assumed personal responsibility for Mr. Bhairam's campaign, though his overall busybodyness unsettled Devan no end. Whenever Lall showed up at the Villa, Devan recalled his father telling him that all businessmen were crooks; he would think this particularly as he watched Lall huddling with Mr. Bhairam as they discussed election strategy. Devan, still smarting from his failure to teach the stable-boys Hindu ethics, didn't want to be left out; standing close by and listening in, he now and again added a few words, usually quotations from his Enmore speech still fresh in his mind. And though Lall and Mr. Bhairam would look questioningly at him when he spoke, Devan was never deterred; he merely grinned at them awkwardly, then, walked back to his room, to be alone, to blot out everything on his mind.

Now he left Punam to look after the horses, and in his room he concentrated on the need for purity of soul, purity of thought, purity of action. The coming election, he reflected, was a significant Hindu event bordering on the sacrosanct since it would decide the fate of the most important Hindu in Guiana, perhaps in the entire Caribbean. These thoughts were with him night and day as he meditated and prayed, from time to time trying another headstand and wobbling semi-perpendicularly. There were times when, with blood purpling his veins, he would hear the loud neighing of the horses, or see the face of the half-veiled woman at Enmore – usually Tara's – and he had to struggle to maintain his posture and think about purity of soul or imagine a throng of people clamouring to vote for Mr. Bhairam. But occasionally, sitting with legs folded in the lotus position, meditating and praying until late at night, there were times when he would no longer hear the horses neighing or the shout and babble of human voices, when he sensed the utmost silence and the peace of *Atman*, a perfect bliss, coming to him, and he listened to the sweet rhythms of his own breathing, feeling as if he was at the Centre of the Universe. Holding his breath for a while he knew then, beyond the shadow of a doubt, that Mr. Bhairam would become the president of the All India League. But sometimes when he held his breath too long, and had to breathe out too quickly, the sensation of momentary darkness frightened him.

The gathering at the League's headquarters on Lamaha Avenue was, of course, larger than usual; everyone was there to hear the election results. The relaxed, holiday spirit of many of those present served only to worsen Devan's state of anxiety. He breathed in hard as he watched Ganesh Lall flitting about from one group to another, and caught sight of Sarwan Singh, calm and suave in a dark suit, looking as if he'd already won the elections. Mr. Bhairam, on the other hand, looked distant, pale, distressed. He looked at Sarwan Singh again and recalled the day the lawyer had visited him at the Preparatory and how officious he had been; now he looked so confident, though there was still a touch of arrogance about him. He watched Sarwan Singh laughing loudly, all eyes turned to him, some laughing agreeably; even Mr. Bhairam turned and looked at the lawyer and was about to laugh too, thought Devan.

'Swami Devan, I presume,' said a smiling figure suddenly before him. Devan, still absorbed with Singh, hung out a hand like a disjointed tentacle as he murmured, 'Yes, yes,' and took in a bald, bespectacled man clad in a Nehru jacket, an imposing figure.

'I am Aurobindo Ghose,' said the man with a distinctly round head, the hair-line receding, the forehead prominent and distinguished.

The smile vanished from Devan's face and his eyes narrowing, he instinctively muttered, 'Bachelor of Arts' – to which Aurobindo Ghose nodded, just sufficiently, like a man used to having his qualifications trumpeted; and Devan asked, as if he had no other choice, 'How's de school going?'

Aurobindo smiled, and Devan noted the handsome round face, the smooth hands, the finely manicured nails and how, when he spoke, his words seemed to come out of his mouth like butter.

'Progress, Swami.' Aurobindo slowly pressed the sleeves of his Nehru jacket, then, in a laconic way, added: 'What d'you think the election results will be?'

'Mr. Bhairam going to win!' Devan blurted in a high pitched squeak, his throat suddenly dry.

'Oh?' Then Aurobindo smiled once more, his handsome face relaxed, unruffled. 'You will be in for a surprise, Swami.'

'Surprise?'

'Yes.'

'Rural voters go vote for Mr. Bhairam,' Devan ventured, finding the full range of his voice now and, because he spoke a little too loudly, a few people turned and looked at him, and one scoffed.

Aurobindo, once more pressing the sleeves of his jacket, murmured, 'Only financial members are allowed to vote.' He wetted his lips as if he was tasting something good, observing the abject discomfort on Devan's face and at how his eyes narrowed as if he was about to start a rapid succession of blinks but wasn't sure when he should begin.

Devan suddenly recalled Gocolram alluding to financial members' privileges, at Enmore, but he'd been too busy looking for Tara to find out more about this. The Principal smiled and quivered happily before leaving Devan, now genuinely anxious, who looked after him and felt a resentment welling up from the very marrow of his bones. He was prevented from dwelling more on this when a voice at the microphone called out for everyone to be seated. Devan looked at the Returning Officer, a man with exceedingly large eyes who wore a checkered grey and white jacket, and his heart beat faster. The official announced:

'The votes have been counted twice and I am ready to announce the results.' He tittered at the microphone, which made a corresponding whistling sound, ending in a mechanical shriek, which caused laughter, followed by calls for hush, indicating the collective eagerness to know the results. Now everyone glanced at Sarwan Singh, then at Mr. Bhairam. Devan was in a daze as he looked forlornly at the Returning Officer – the official's eyes seemed to brighten and grow long, like fluorescent bulbs – and he appeared to be looking directly at him as he commented on the fairness of the elections and how the All India League had always been blessed with outstanding leaders; how there was no other such organisation in the Caribbean, not even in Surinam where there were lots of East Indians; how it had been a fiercely fought election campaign (with elements of sleaze, he hinted), but this only indicated the calibre of the contestants. Everyone laughed and Devan saw Lall scurry on the spot and Aurobindo smugly lighting a pipe and sucking at it as if about to swallow it whole. A glitter emanated from Sarwan Singh now, and Devan quickly looked from him to the paleness of Mr. Bhairam.

Devan watched transfixed as the Returning Officer moved closer to the microphone, coughing dramatically for effect, like a man who enjoyed keeping everyone in suspense, shutting his eyes like doors to blot out the light, then opening them again. They were now merely empty sockets staring back as he solemnly announced:

'Results of elections for president of our august All India League are as follows.' He coughed again, attempting a grand manner, but looking like a deformed stork as he pulled his head back, continuing only after an appropriate murmur from the crowd. 'Candidate number one, Mr. Bhairam Bhuraji – long-standing member, forty-five years of age–' Again he stopped and cleared his throat as if he'd had phlegm thick as glue caught at the back of it since his infancy. Devan also cleared his throat in instinctive imitation.

'Five hundred and seventy votes.'

Loud applause followed, the sound like a short squall of rain. Devan glanced at Mr. Bhairam, at how excited he seemed, how his eyes lit up; then he looked at Ganesh Lall whose expression was the complete opposite: one of intense worry. Devan felt the same expression spread across to his own face and he closed his eyes tightly as the Returning Officer, grinning, as if he knew something no-one else did, continued more slowly:

'Candidate Number Two, Mr. Sarwan Singh, long-standing member and barrister-at-law, age forty-two... number of votes polled... NINE HUNDRED AND FORTY FIVE!'

Tremendous applause broke from Singh's supporters, who seemed to be everywhere in the hall; who shouted at the top of their voices more vociferously each moment that went on, calling out to each other as if they had all gone berserk. Amidst this din Devan felt an intense shiver ripping through his body leaving him numb, ice-cold; in this state he watched Aurobindo shake the lawyer's hand, no longer placid and aloof but a robust and gregarious creature who could do nothing else but keep pumping the victor's arm, intent it seemed on taking it out of its socket. The Returning Officer also expressed congratulations, but he seemed only to be talking to the microphone because the applause still resounded and it wasn't until the outgoing president, the frail Nakeram Harresh, took the podium that order was restored.

But Devan no longer listened; he figured now he'd never be a member of the All India League. He felt wretched, alone, and unconsciously he looked around for Gocolram; then the need to be away from everyone overwhelmed him and he looked about for a small room – even a washroom – where he could be by himself, though he knew that in Georgetown the washrooms were unlike the outhouses in the rural areas where one could sit for hours and meditate and feel cut off from the rest of human activity for a while. When he couldn't find anywhere to escape to, he found himself gravitating towards Mr. Bhairam. 'Bad luck,' he muttered in a barely audible tone to his benefactor, but the latter laughed, his face surprisingly animated. 'Well, Swami, Sarwan Singh will do a fine job. I am not a public speaker anyway.'

'But you a man of action,' protested Devan, puzzled. Mr. Bhairam chuckled like a child who was being given a toy. 'Ah, Swami, I am a Hindu, I must be a good loser.' The child's chuckle gave way to a bark of laughter; Devan watched in amazement. In the same mood he watched Mr. Bhairam go to the microphone where he talked about the fairness of the elections and, expressing his congratulations to the lawyer, stressed that a Hindu must always be a good loser. When he laughed again, Devan could not help feeling that it was Mr. Bhairam's destiny to be a good loser.

It was Singh's turn at the microphone, and he strutted confidently to it and, without gloating over his victory, he talked in a measured tone for nearly an hour, thanking everyone, and outlining his various plans as the new president of the League, including plans for further extending the Georgetown Preparatory. Then he praised a number of people, including Aurobindo Ghose, and concluded:

'Let me thank all my supporters once more, staunch Hindus as they all are; you have shown beyond a shadow of a doubt that you have great confidence in me, and this is seen clearly in the margin of victory.' He smiled, and with a bare hint of gloating, the only time he really did this, added: 'I thank you all again for putting me at the helm where our dear Nakeram Harresh has served so well. Rest assured that no one will be disappointed in me.' Then the lawyer spent another ten minutes lavishing praises on the outgoing president, whose frail figure throbbed as the adulation was interspersed with clapping. When Singh stepped down from the podium, Mr. Bhairam was among the first to start long and generous applause.

Devan also applauded, though mechanically; he still yearned to be in a cubicle by himself, and he didn't care that further results were being announced: that Aurobindo Ghose became treasurer, and N.R. Goshan became secretary, and P.M. Shaw became...

Ganesh Lall, appearing as if from nowhere, cried with hot breath in Devan's ears, 'Unfair elections, Swami!'

'Financial members,' Devan replied, calmly.

Lall wouldn't be put off, insisting that the elections were unfair, that there were too many spoilt votes and irregularities. 'I tell you, Swamiji, how else can you explain defeat?' He glowered at Devan and seemed about to pound at his chest, but Devan remained obdurately disconsolate and nothing that Lall said could shake him out of this mood.

Devan now rarely saw Mr. Bhairam at the Villa; they seemed to be on separate paths. Devan remained in his room, and each time Punam came to him to tell him how the horses were doing he smelled strong incense and concluded that the trainer was going into a new phase of a swami's life – which he wanted to tell the others about. But he knew they would only laugh and he decided to keep this to himself.

Devan's only other visitor was Mrs. Bhairam, who still came to his room as before; she was the only one he really talked to. 'Where is Mr. Bhairam?' he asked softly, almost whispering.

'Gone to the rural areas, Swami,' she replied equally softly.

'What for?'

'Ah, Swamiji, my husband is a very sentimental man. He loves people, you see; he's not gloomy because he lost the election.' She looked a little sternly at him now. 'Besides, I don't think he seriously wanted to become president of the All India League.'

'Oh?'

Mrs. Bhairam uttered a short laugh but she didn't say more, except, 'There's a lot to learn about Bhai you know,' and left. Devan returned to the familiar corner of his room, thoughts of the defeat recurring like an old sickness. Again he recalled Gocolram talking about financial members, and he regretted not getting the Mahaica pandit to expand on it. Next he began to wonder if Gocolram indeed had a hand in Mr. Bhairam's defeat, and when Lall called upon him, he told him what he thought. But Lall merely repeated his charges, 'They have cheated us, Swami. Take my word for it, they have! Voting by financial members is a recent – a new – regulation brought about by Sarwan Singh a month before the elections!'

'Why didn't Mr. Bhairam object?' Devan asked tiredly.

The other didn't answer, he merely continued: 'We mustn't allow him to get away with this.' And Devan, his thoughts still on Gocolram, and then on Mr. Bhairam in the rural areas, imagined what it would be like to receive plentiful gifts of fruit, spices, and money all over again. He smiled as Lall thrust out his hands towards his chest as if he didn't know what else to do with them. But when an image of Mrs. Gocolram appeared before Devan, the smile changed to a heavy scowl – as he looked at Lall, to hear him say with a new-found clarity in his voice, 'We must mek sure Destiny win at all cost!'

'Destiny, eh?'

'Yes, yes, Swami!'

But the scowl remained on Devan's face like a permanent imprint, and as he continued looking at Lall he muttered the horse's name over and over again; even when Lall scurried out, leaving behind a scent of tweed, Devan was still muttering the horse's name like a mantra.

FIFTEEN

Mr. Bhairam retired to the tower and took to playing the harmonium incessantly; its strains spread all over the building, even to the stables when it was quiet. There the stable-boys, hearing the sounds, would jiggle their bodies in mock harmony. Mrs. Bhairam, escaping from the upper floor of the Villa, confided to Devan, 'See, Swamiji, my husband is a very sentimental man.' Devan closed his eyes and it seemed his ears correspondingly opened, causing a louder strain of the music to fill his head. He quickly opened his eyes and looked at her, and she smiled bravely. 'When he's not on the East Coast, Bhai only sits before the harmonium, night and day. Oh, now I can hardly even talk to you; he's always around with the harmonium sounding everywhere.' She said this in a regretful tone, and Devan was flattered: he stretched out a hand towards her, but she drew back at once.

When she walked away, Devan looked at her body, how it swayed a little; but quickly chided himself for allowing the senses to govern his mind; and he forced himself to dwell nostalgically on his days in Mahaica.

Devan would have been surprised if he had known that at that very time, Gocolram – in his familiar sanctum – was thinking seriously about whether Mr. Bhairam would continue to make donations to the Mahaica Hindu Temple, and whether he would give funds towards the building of a preparatory close by. Gocolram really wished for the latter, since he felt he might become the principal and enjoy privileges similar to Aurobindo's – he no longer enjoyed the wear and tear of a pandit's life, especially the bicycling in his dhoti, the flowing robe getting into the spokes of the wheels from time to time as he attended one puja or jhandi after another. These endless religious ceremonies left him jaded. A principal's lot would be more fulfilling; then he would get respect from Christians, Muslims and everyone else, including the Africans, who seemed good at education because they dominated the teaching profession, though in schools run by the Christians. And he imagined himself in a Nehru jacket similar to Aurobindo's walking around proprietorially without the pretence of sanctimony, which was also a severe burden. He was concerned too about the education of his own children; as a principal, he'd be able to supervise their learning himself.

He went to his wife in the lower flat to ask her what she thought Mr. Bhairam might do, and whether he, as influential pandit of Mahaica, should give his support to the new president of the All India League. He valued his wife's practical sense. She scowled at his indecision, as the children caterwauled round her; she agreed that he should do just that, support Sarwan Singh. 'He a lawyer, no?' she asserted. And Gocolram wasted no time in drafting a letter to Sarwan Singh, with his wife supervising, a child in her arms bawling from time to time. Gocolram began by congratulating the lawyer on his recent victory, then pledged the full support of the rural Hindus. The pandit also contemplated writing to Aurobindo Ghose, thinking that if he ingratiated himself sufficiently with the latter, he might become a close friend.

'It tek a great mind to be a Sanskrit scholar, eh?' Gocolram said, still thinking about Aurobindo. But Mrs. Gocolram just scowled, clutching their youngest child who was bawling loudly, as if he'd swallowed a wiri-wiri pepper – leaving Gocolram to feel that she had no interest in the finer things in life.

Devan asked Lall, 'You tink Pandit Gocolram have a hand in the irregularities?'

'One can never be too careful, Swami.' The businessman knew very well that Devan's attitude towards the Mahaica pandit see-sawed. 'Maybe he shoulda warn us dat the rural members were not financial.'

Devan's eyelids fluttered as he looked at Lall, who confided, 'Human nature's evil, Swami.' And both of them silently contemplated the profundity of this observation. Then to break their gloom, Devan muttered, 'Destiny boun' to win.'

Lall laughed and repeated Devan's phrase; then they repeated it together, to the strains of Mr. Bhairam's harmonium which had suddenly became louder. 'Yes, Swami, dat's it – it bound to win.'

'It must?' Devan asked, as if he no longer believed it. Again the strains of the harmonium rose, resounding everywhere. 'Yes, yes,' replied Lall, 'it must win.'He got up, hurrying away, chased it seemed by the sounds from the harmonium rising in crescendo. Devan laughed as he pictured Lall's footsteps retreating, imagining the businessman racing down the streets of Georgetown in his small car, muttering, 'Irregularities... Destiny boun' to win!'

The stable-boys, outside, hearing the sounds of the harmonium, showed their appreciation by jiggling their bodies. Punam tried to explain. 'You see, Mr. Bhairam become really sad since the election results. Dat's what Swami Devan say.' They laughed, jiggling their bodies lewdly. Close by a horse neighed, but it sounded far away, like a distant cry of pain. One of the boys said, 'Maybe Mr. Bhairam turning a swami too jus' like Devan, eh?'

'Na, it na true,' another said. 'Is impossible because he too fat to stand pon he head.'

As the sounds of the harmonium rose and then fell, the boys continued chaffing Punam about Mr. Bhairam. Another said, 'Maybe Mr. Bhai really go become a musician.'

Punam countered, in ever loyal fashion, 'Mr. Bhairam is a man of fine taste. Swamiji himself say so.'

Further laughter, and Boysie said: 'Maybe it is the Swami's madness catching on to he. He go bring Mr. Bhairam to disgrace, you see. It would never be that way with Mr. Athan.'

'Mr. Athan is a Christian,' replied Punam hotly. 'He should never be here.'

'Is dat what Devan said?' countered another of the boys.

Punam looked flustered, he didn't know what to answer.

And another said, 'What if Mr. Athan is a Jew, eh? What if, eh?'

Punam looked even more flustered, and Boysie said, 'Guiana is not India. We not only have Hindus living here. We got all races an' religions mixing.'

'Indians are de majority,' answered Punam, recovering his composure.

'What about Muslims?' countered another with Muslim relatives.

'Hindus are the majority. Go to the countryside, you go see; they all like Mr. Bhairam.'

'How come he didn't win de elections then?' asked Boysie.

'It was unfair,' said Punam.

'Who tol' you dat?' another of the boys quizzed.

'Me uncle. He hear Swami speech at Enmore; it was a good speech he say too. Rural Hindus always vote for Mr. Bhairam.'

The others looked at Punam and, not sure how to respond, they laughed; coming closer round him they pressed, 'Swami Devan tell you dat too?

'Yes, yes,' Punam replied, defiantly, on the verge of tears, which was what the others were expecting, wanting to happen.

'Is that why Mr. Bhairam hire Swami Devan? Because he comes from Providence Village in Berbice, eh? Because he's a coolie like all the others, eh?' They sniggered, laughed again, and Punam, his ears red with anger, fighting back the tears, blurted out, 'Swami's father is a respected man; he come from India! He not just a coolie!'

'Oh?'

'What's his name?' asked Govind.

'Gautum Lall Chattergoon.'

And like a familiar practised refrain, the others mimicked, 'Chattergoon, Chattergoon! Baboon! Baboon!' And to the loud accompaniment of the harmonium they jiggled their bodies and laughed. Punam watched them in frenzy and anxiety. They too watched him, not without some admiration for his loyalty. As the music died down, another sound rose, a loud neighing, coming from Destiny's stable. They all knew something was the matter, and they hurried to find out, in a show of loyalty all their own. They saw Devan standing almost trance-like before the horse, a tense expression on his face, oblivious of their presence, a newspaper in his hand. He'd been reading how well the Syndicate horses were doing at gallops and had come to see Destiny to reassure himself. And the strains of the music swelled again, the harmonium now seeming independent even of Mr. Bhairam, rising and falling when it felt like it.

Devan turned and looked at the horse, and muttered to himself, 'Boun' to win.'

Laughter. Devan, hearing them, laughed himself, because Destiny would indeed win. The Syndicate horses would never be able to win against him, and he was telling them that, challenging their doubt, each one now looking at the horse as it turned around. Then the horse stopped, and remained still and watched them. Each one. And they laughed again to break the tension when the horse once more neighed, snorted. Their laughter infuriated Devan, and he blurted out, 'No ethics!'

The boys, as if in one voice, cried out, 'Chattergoon, Chattergoon! Baboon, Baboon!' Punam felt dismayed, as never before: he drew closer to the horse, his loyalty still intact. Devan, watching them and coming out of his trance-like state, hurried away, thinking they were beyond redemption, rascals and agents of the devil.

'They ought to be fired!' He told Mr. Bhairam as he bumped into him coming down the stairs.

'Who?'

'The rascals– out dere!' He pointed, his arm shooting out as if about to be disjointed from its socket.

Mr. Bhairam, refusing to be taken aback – he knew his trainer only too well – said firmly, 'But the October meeting is only a month away, Swami.'

'Never mind!'

'Never mind?' Mr. Bhairam asked feebly now, starting to frown laboriously. Devan nodded and Mr. Bhairam rushed back up the stairs to the tower to seek the refuge of his harmonium. On the way he bumped into his wife who, seeing his agitated look, anxiously asked, 'What's the matter, Bhai?'

'The boys – they're giving Swami Devan a hard time.'

'Oh, poor Swamiji,' she moaned. 'They shouldn't do that to him. He's a man of God. Our young generation is so worthless.'

Later, while the harmonium played, Mrs. Bhairam repeated to Devan, 'Worth-less, worth-less!'

SIXTEEN

Excitement was extremely high about the coming race meeting along the East and West coasts of Demerara. Rumour had it that the entire county of Berbice was in ferment, especially in the Corentyne district of Port Mourant where most East Indians lived (and which was the breeding ground of several notable politicians, including a firebrand Communist and another who, self-exiled in London, made loud noises at Hyde Park each Sunday). In Essequibo, the third and largest county but the least populated, there was very little enthusiasm, though in the rice-growing district of Wakenaam, everyone talked about Mr. Bhairam's chances with Destiny. Many had heard of Swami Devan as an orator but few could understand his role as a trainer of race horses, though die-hard Hindus, often much older than the rest, were intrigued, their cynicism giving way to enthusiasm, and they began to follow the race news keenly.

In Georgetown itself, the enthusiasm began to gather steam only slowly. Once or twice Pandit Gocolram came to the capital and returned to Mahaica but with only a little news about the upcoming meeting, though everyone thought he would have much to add to the heated discussion about Mr. Bhairam's chances. What they didn't know was that Gocolram was visiting Aurobindo Ghose at the Georgetown Preparatory and even seeing Sarwan Singh when the latter wasn't too busy. Back in Mahaica though, trying to escape the boredom of a pandit's life, Gocolram was never too far away from the rum-shops, listening in on the heated arguments about the race meeting, muttering to anyone who asked for his opinion, 'Keen rivalry, dat's all.' But when someone reeking of X-M rum cried out, 'Sarwan Singh co-operatin' wid Christians an' Muslims! How can it be, eh?' the pandit replied, 'All men are brothers,' and fled the drunks.

At the Villa, Mr. Bhairam, now beginning to get over his loss at the recent League elections and thinking of another large donation he would make to the East Coast Hindus, pressed hard on the keys of his harmonium, making the instrument moan loudly.

In his room Devan heard the chord and frowned; Punam continued with his report about the practice sessions at the D'Urban Park race track. 'Destiny doing well, Swami. Have no fear. Before long he go be in top form.'

'Top form, eh?'

'Yes-yes,' Punam's eyes gleamed.

'Keep riding him you'self. No other. Don't let the other boys go near him at all.'

'Why not, Swami?' In the past the other stable boys had always accompanied him to the race track to record the gallops.

'They are worthless.'

Punam thought about this for a moment. 'What about race-day, Swami?'

'Race-day?'

'Yes. Who'll ride Destiny?'

'You will – you will!' Devan cried out harshly, unconsciously waiting to hear another chord from the harmonium, which didn't in fact come, leaving Punam to think that he wasn't a licensed jockey and had never ridden Destiny in a race before. But Devan kept insisting that only he must ride Destiny, adding that Ganesh Lall would see to it that he received a license in time.

'But... Swami,' interjected Punam, still not sure, though the thought of riding Mr. Bhairam's champion horse in an actual race had always excited him; now was his chance, and he was flattered by Devan's faith in him.

The next day Devan, after reading another report in the newspaper about how the horses from the Syndicate were doing at gallops, decided to go with Punam to the racetrack. Punam was pleased that he was showing more interest.

'You gon' like it there,Swami,' said Punam.But the race track immediately made Devan feel uncomfortable. He stood sniffing a little and looking at the horses from the Syndicate sprinting down the paddocks at what seemed a breathtaking speed. Devan grew even more uncomfortable and alarmed as he watched the many Africans and others of mixed race around, loudly applauding their favourites or heckling the opposition. 'Have no fear, Swami, it alright. Destiny does go faster – you'll see,' Punam said, as he approached holding Mr. Bhairam's champion horse by the bridle.

'Eh?' replied Devan, still looking at the track, vaguely imagining Gosai's filly. No, it was impossible, Gosai's filly wouldn't be able to run so fast; it was a horse meant only for brushing and currying. But Destiny snorted, its eyes focusing on Devan and growing larger each moment. Devan, reluctantly, nervously, joined Punam in holding its bridle, the sound of thundering hooves in his ears increasing his apprehension.

Then two reporters spotted the champion horse and, to their delight, Devan, the mysterious Hindu trainer. Their note pads fluttering in their hands, one jutted a pencil in Devan's face. 'What d'you tink of the Syndicate horses, Swami?' Devan looked at the paddock, looked at the next horse sprinting down the tracks; he wasn't sure what to reply, he mumbled something... about Destiny... and the reporters scribbled furiously, one grinning. Devan didn't like the look on his face; he wished they would ask about Destiny instead of the Syndicate's horses. He squirmed, as they wrote more. 'Syndicate haas, eh?' he repeated to himself, his discomfort increasing.

'Yes, Don Dinero – he's the fastest. Can Destiny win against him?'

'Don...' he started, looking at the track, not sure which one was Don Dinero. Was it the big bay colt? Was it the red one sprinting the last three furlongs at breakneck speed? He looked at Punam, who held on to Destiny tightly.

'Haven't you heard of Don Dinero before, Swami?' asked another reporter. 'He used to race at Arima in Trinidad, you know.'

'Arima, eh?'

Laughter; and Punam looked anxiously at Devan, thinking it was time that Mr. Bhairam's champion horse started its training. But Devan still held the horse by the bridle as the reporters scribbled on, highly amused. Punam wasn't sure what to do next, and he pulled Destiny a little towards him, causing the horse to snort, and Devan, taken by surprise, leapt to one side. Again the reporters laughed. Devan, embarrassed, hollered, 'You are all agents of the Devil! Get away! Get away from him! From Destiny!'

The reporters looked at each other in amazement, scribbling delightedly in their pads. And Devan remembered, too clearly now, what the newspapers had written about him in the past: how incensed he'd been. Incensed again, his eyes swirling as he jerked at Destiny's bridle, he hurried away from the track, leaving Punam running behind and feebly protesting: 'Wait, wait, Panditji! Destiny got to run today; he got to practice. Mr Athan used to say dat; everyday from now on.'

Devan, letting go of the horse, hurried away from the paddocks: to be away from the reporters; to be far away from the Syndicate horses as well. He knew from now on he would merely rely on Punam's reports to him each day on how Destiny was doing at gallops.

Back at the Villa, Devan met Mr. Bhairam, who seemed surprisingly less morose and harmonium-bound.

'You heard about it, Swamiji?' asked Mr. Bhairam, sprightly, delighted by something.

'Heard what?' replied Devan, the paddocks, the reporters, the Syndicate horses, Destiny, the horses racing down the track still in his mind's eye.

'There's going to be a match race.'

'A what... ?' Devan looked confused, thundering hooves still echoing in his mind.

'A match-race, Swamiji. The Syndicate wants to run

their best horse against my Destiny; two horses alone, you understand. No other horse to interfere at the gates or on the rails. The two best horses, the two fastest. Everyone will be excited by it, everyone, yes!' Mr. Bhairam continued smiling, he wanted his trainer to express enthusiasm now.

But Devan merely asked, as if still in the throes of doubt, 'Their best haas?'

'Don Dinero, yes. You've heard about it, haven't you, Swami?'

Devan closed his eyes, his thoughts swimming, back at the tracks: Don Dinero, the reporters' questions, pencils scribbling, hooves thundering.

But Mr. Bhairam was a man awakened from a long harmonium-ridden sleep. 'A one-to-one race, Swamiji. It will be history, the first of its kind at D'Urban Park, you understand. Everyone will watch Destiny run at full speed – and run to victory! Now they will know, the whole world will know' – by which he meant the entire Caribbean – 'they will see what my horse can do, Hindu as I am; I will now be a real winner, not a loser!' He emphasised the words 'winner' and 'loser', and laughed. Devan watched him in amazement, not sure what he should say. Mr. Bhairam added, 'I hear Sarwan Singh is putting up a lot of money in a bet with me.'

'A bet?'

'Yes. I must take him on, eh? To save my honour, Swamiji.'

'Honour?' Devan asked under his breath, looking fixedly at Mr. Bhairam, not sure he was hearing correctly, as he thought of ethics, right behaviour – phrases from Hindu scripture coming to him as Mr. Bhairam tittered, like a child.

'Ethics,' Devan said, in an inane rhetorical way, as if it was a foreign word, with foreign implications; nothing to do with him, or Mr. Bhairam; or Hindus; or anyone else for that matter. And he too brightened and laughed.

At Enmore, Tara's interest in what Devan was doing grew day by day; she heard about the upcoming race-meeting and the match-race everyone was talking about. Yet she couldn't come to grips with the idea that Devan was indeed Mr. Bhairam's trainer. 'He never goin' give up meditating,' she repeated to herself, then to her relatives, and to her children, one by one. Her son Jotish looked at her, then made a coarse sound of disgust with his mouth, a cross between a clack and an arrested whistle. Tara rebuked him at once, 'Stop suckin' yuh teet'!' Her daughters, Shanti and Devi, watched sheepishly, their braided black hair showing wayward strands which the comb had failed to pull neatly into place.

The relatives, looking at her and the children, murmured, 'Is not right for a Hindu wife to be away from her husband.'

She sensed that their concern with her marriage had grown with the news of Devan's fame. They were eager to know about him since his association with Mr. Bhairam and the talk of his gifts as a speaker on the East Coast hadn't escaped them. But she looked askance when they added, 'A Hindu wife must bear she chafe. Maybe being with haas go mek he practical now. He boun' to change.'

But Tara had other thoughts, chiefly the image of Devan still praying, meditating, and she replied, 'Yes, I go have to bear me chafe, dat's all.' Right then Jotish sucked his teeth again, and Tara let fly a sharp slap against his ears. Jotish, smarting, with face awry, cried out, 'I go tell he! I go tell me daddy what you do!'

'Go now, you ingrate!' Tara fired back at him.

The relatives watched this violence between mother and son with mild awe and said to Jotish: 'Boy, you mus' obey you modder; you see how she tek care o' you. She got to bear she chafe.' Jotish instinctively sucked his teeth again and ran outside like a regular vagrant. The girls, Shanti and Devi, tittered loudly, and Tara shook her head dolefully, as if all was lost.

Alone, Tara reflected on her husband. The thought of

bearing her chafe for the rest of her life made her quiver with resentment. Yet, her ears perked up when she heard Devan's name mentioned once or twice on the radio, and she listened keenly to what was said, her heart thumping a little; it was as if her own name was being mentioned. The relatives, overhearing it too, would rush up to her with excitement, 'Tara, you hear dat? You hear? They callin' Devan's name. You husban' prappa famous now, eh? Just t'ink how Lachandai an' Chattergoon go be glad to hear he name; they must be really happy,' and they laughed, excitement and cynical amusement evenly mixed.

Tara, pretending she hadn't heard, was disdainful. But when, once in a while, she looked at the newspaper, she found herself searching for his picture in it. Then the relatives in mock-rebuke would say, 'Gal-Tara, you na can read. You only look at photograph? You tink you go see you husband picture?' Tara would hurriedly throw aside the newspaper, but her daughters Shanti and Devi, then Jotish, would snatch it up, searching the print for their father's name. Everyone else would look in amazement at the intensity in the children's eyes, how like floodlights they shone, how deep was Jotish's concentration. Tara, though, still tried to disguise the intense longing she felt to see her husband again. Indeed, she wasn't sure if the longing really derived from a lingering affection or nostalgia for him or merely from curiosity. But the relatives guessed how she felt, and they chaffed her for being the wife of a swami-turned-race-horse-trainer. It was Tara's turn now to suck her teeth, even more loudly than Jotish, who, overhearing, burst out laughing in unbridled gladness. Even her daughters laughed. It was then as she watched them that Tara was sure that she would see her husband before long. She sensed too that Devan was probably having to answer questions about her and the children from those curious about his past; this seemed inevitable the more she thought about it, and before she could catch herself she started weeping.

And indeed at the Villa, Mrs. Bhairam was saying to

Devan in her most confidential tone, 'Tell me more about your family, Swamiji.' She smiled, inviting him to indulge his nostalgia, to accept the family side in him, Hindu as he was, even though he was a man devoted totally to their beloved religion.

Devan had long feared that she might ask him about this, and feigning a look of anguish, replied, 'She is a devoted woman, my wife; I miss she. Me son, too.'

This touched Mrs. Bhairam as she took full note of the pained expression on his face; indeed, she thought, how lonely he must be in his great sacrifice, and, sentimental as she was, she asked: 'What did she look like on her wedding day?'

'Oh, radiant,' he replied, his thoughts going to that special day when he'd listened to the Tarlogie pandit; he recalled too how he'd tried peeping at Tara behind her veil, and looking directly at Mrs. Bhairam, he added: 'but covered from head to toe.'

Mrs. Bhairam assumed a rueful expression of her own and dabbing at a mist of tears with the tail-end of her sari, said: 'Ah, our custom, Swamiji.'

Devan, trying his best, managed a sad but winning smile.

SEVENTEEN

'Who is it?'

'Is me... Punam.'

'You mus' na come here at dis time,' said Devan, eyes closed, legs folded, sitting in the middle of his room, ready for intense meditation. He didn't want to be disturbed, not now. A few moments ago he'd blotted out all sounds, forced himself not to think of the horses neighing, whinnying.

'But is important, Swamiji.'

'What is?' he asked, irascibly, eyes still closed, concentrating harder. Perfect bliss, he thought, no horses now, no sound; he had an inkling of it right here in Georgetown, this place so far away from India, this country close to the Orinoco; here, the infinite recesses of the Universe, the Great Consciousness. Soon he would be at one with the Omniscient, the Creator of the World. He breathed the names of Brahma and Krishna. God by any other name was the same, wasn't it? Lord... Jehovah, Christ, Moses, Buddha, Mohammed; a pantheon of Hindu deities raced across his mind, deities in all forms, avatars, including Hanuman, the monkey-God, in all manner of acts; a god eavesdropping and in a playful mood as he watched the nubile cow-girls bathing and giggling happily in their embarrassment; deities clapping hands and singing bhajans. What else? The psalms of Solomon and David echoed in his mind from his childhood days at school. He fought to control this turbulence of belief, faith, India and Guiana: past and present see-sawing in his mind. He concentrated harder against the neighing of the horses.

'Destiny, Swami – he lame!'

Devan jumped up, surprised that Punam was still there,

and he felt that in that moment all the deities who had been with him had fled, leaving him in perturbed aloneness. 'Impossible,' he cried.

'Is true. I notice him dis morning.'

'Is na true,' he continued like a man greatly wronged, his face a paroxysm of distress, teeth chattering as he bolted out of his room to the stables, Punam close behind, explaining, apologising.

'Right leg or left?' Devan asked in a flurry.

'Right.'

'How it happen?'

'I don't know; maybe at gallops yesterday, Swami.'

'Gallops, eh?'

'Yes, yes.'

Devan thought at once of the onlookers at the racetrack, a bewitched place, of the reporters, followers of the Syndicate, non-Hindus all of them: they were everywhere he turned; they perpetrated this; they were all enemies – dire ones, he cried out, like a man goaded to the point of madness. And with a deeper paroxysm overtaking his face Devan added, 'You mustn' let anybody know about this!'

'Nobody?'

'Nobody.'

Puzzlement on the boy's face, growing consternation: Punam wasn't sure what to do or say. 'What about Mr. Bhairam, Swami?' he finally asked.

'Not even he!' snapped Devan.

For the first time Punam wondered if Boysie and the other stable-boys might be right in their assessment of the trainer. He watched Devan bend over, leaning forward, reaching out, examining the horse's right leg for a while, then going much closer. The horse stirred, and stepped back. Devan looked at Punam for a second, then stretched out once more towards the horse: Punam wasn't sure what he was inspecting... 'Maybe it get better in a couple of days' time,' Devan murmured.

Punam nodded in a quick conciliatory way; he was

alarmed, despite his belief in the swami. He did not want to feel this way, but when Devan added, with eyes swirling, 'We mus' have faith in God!' and hurried back to his room, muttering, 'Enemies, enemies!' Punam was perplexed as never before.

He returned to Destiny's stable and looked at the horse's leg for a good hour, wracking his mind over what he should do. Maybe he should tell Boysie, who knew more about horses than himself. But Swamiji didn't want him to tell anyone. He mustn't. No one! He stared up at the windows of the Villa for a while and wondered if Mr. Bhairam was still playing the harmonium and what his reaction would be if he were to discover that Destiny was lame. 'Pray to God,' he thought, Swami's words echoing in his mind. He turned, looked at the horse and patted it on its forehead. Maybe the injury would go away in a couple of days' time.

When Destiny wasn't seen at the gallops it began to be rumoured that Devan was using wizardry as part of his training method; this made people all the more intrigued. Ganesh Lall read the allusion to this in the newspapers, grimaced, then laughed. Putting the newspaper aside he drove at once to Vlissengen, grinning all the while; wizardry indeed.

Devan opened the door to see the businessman's wide smile, to hear his enquiry, to be told the rumour of wizardry. 'Rascals,' let out Devan. 'They's rascals.'

Lall by now knew the swami's reactions to most things so he took no notice of his agitation and grinned. 'Don't worry with the boys at the stables, or the reporters. They just rascals, true-true?'

But when at Lall's insistence, Devan took him to see Destiny, the businessman called out in horror, 'It is lame!' For a moment even he was silenced. But then he recovered his positive manner and chirped, 'You must leave it to me, eh Swami. I getting the vet to look at Destiny's foot. It will be okay in no time.' Devan was offended that Destiny's recovery was no longer to be entrusted to the hands of God, but he was also secretly relieved that the responsibility had been taken from him. Lall, noting his doubt, added, 'It is just a match-race, Swami, eh. Only two haases running; it'll be easy for Destiny, see. The vet mek sure he win.'

Devan's feelings were still in a see-saw state when Lall sped off, and he went to the stables once more, looking around, doubt gnawing at him. Then he saw the graffiti, large letters written with chalk, words staring back at him as if they'd always been there – DEVAN DOPES HORSES! A sharp pain seared his breast, anger boiling in him, uncontrollably.

'I go show them!' he cried softly to himself, then loudly, his words grating in his ears. 'Come out! Come out from where you are hiding!' he ranted, and eventually the boys started coming out. Govind was snickering, but Boysie was serious-faced; he sensed the distraught trainer's mammoth wrath. He motioned the others to be silent. Devan pointed at the graffiti and demanded to know who had written the words. In a corner Punam flinched, looking at each of the boys, then at Swami Devan. 'Who? I mus' know. Tell me now!' Devan kept insisting, fingers pointing, accusing each one, including Punam. And the boys feigned innocence, they sneered and laughed again despite Boysie's caution; then he too sneered, as if it was the thing to do in the circumstances. They denied any knowledge of the words. A mysterious hand wrote them, one muttered under his breath; and yet another said, 'Is a Hindu god who wrote the words.' More snickers followed, as Devan's arms swung like a windmill gone haywire.

Mrs. Bhairam, opportunely looking down at the stables from the top storey, saw Devan's windmill gestures, though for a second she couldn't believe her eyes. Devan was advancing closer to the boys, to Boysie, whose fists were balled. Alarmed, she rushed to the her husband and cried out, 'Quick, Bhai! Quick, you must go and look!' The harmoniumist stirred reluctantly, but when he finally looked out, saw the balled fists, hands flailing, he grimaced and hurried downstairs. He arrived just in time to hear Devan saying, 'You tink I is a doper, eh? Well, I go have you backsides fired! Fired – all o' you!'

Devan saw his benefactor and pointed mutely to the graffiti; he was spent, he didn't know what else to say. And slowly the boys walked back to the various stables, Punam last of all, leaving Bhairam and Devan staring at each other, two solitary figures left on stage in a drama where they were the only victims. Then Mr. Bhairam took Devan's arm and guided him into the house.

Upstairs in the Villa, Mrs. Bhairam uttered to her husband – for Devan's benefit, 'They're worthless, those boys! Always worthless!' But Bhairam merely pressed the keys of his harmonium like a man eternally without an audience, without use of words; the instrument his only witness, his only voice.

Later, when Devan told the ubiquitous Lall about the incident, the businessman bristled with an excitement which Devan found puzzling.

'That's the answer, Swamiji!'

'Answer?'

'Yes, yes. You na see; it's the answer to the irregularities. That's how we can get back at Sarwan Singh. You forget about the wrong-doing at the election, eh? Irregularities!' Lall screeched.

Devan drew back, feeling tired; he studied Lall, starting with the familiar forehead, but being surprised at Lall's mouth, how it widened and seemed capable of barking. 'Leave everything to me, Swami,' said the businessman. 'In three days from now, on race day, Destiny going feel good–you see!' He'll run faster than Mr. Bhairam's Mercedes. '

Devan felt he was in the grip of the businessman, that he was being squeezed to smithereens.

'But the foot?' muttered Devan feebly, still withering before Lall who seemed to be growing taller.

'Think nothing of it. Just keep giving it more exercise. It go win.'

'Win, eh?' Devan responded abstractedly.

'Dr. Chu, you see, he prappa good.'

'But... he a pharmacist – not a vet,' Devan muttered, silently, to himself. He forced every ounce of will left in him to look Lall in the eyes: to see him laughing, and growing taller, inch by inch, taking over the room; Lall with many hands, many faces, like a deity, and the faces, each one, were all laughing. Devan rubbed his eyes as if he wanted scales to drop from them.

But Lall was gone. Only Punam stood before him now, the gentle faced boy who would yet make a pandit. 'I will ride Destiny, Swami,' Punam said. 'Mr. Lall tell me, but I riding him only because you want me to.' Punam waited for an acknowledgement, a glint of enthusiasm in Devan's eyes, but he merely nodded.

EIGHTEEN

The D'Urban Park race track sweltered. Though from close up to the pavilion one could see its dilapidated boards jutting out here and there, from a distance the white building shimmered grandly and its rows of seats floated down to the field as in a watery haze. The whole park was surrounded by lush trees, their leaves glistening like filigree and rustling when a gust of wind blew, tempering the heat. A vast concourse of people sweated underneath a brilliant sky, its blueness scarcely etched by scant cirrus clouds drifting just slightly, bunched like cotton wool and sloping for a moment to the wayward eye. Of course, everyone knew that these same clouds could suddenly darken, could become ominous, pregnant with rain; but no one really thought of this now. Only the horses were on their minds, and two horses in particular, titans on hooves.

They had become symbols of good and evil for some of the Hindus; one on the side of Hinduism, the other on the side of all the other forces of a collective evil. Muslims sought out other Muslims and sided with the non-Muslim Sarwan Singh. Christians, usually Afro-Guianese (with only a few Georgetown East Indians among them, who, like the Africans, wore ties close to their necks as if they were constantly engaged in the ritual of throttling themselves) also supported the Syndicate. Closer to race-time everyone would be brought together into one bunched knot until the two horses speeding along would set them free, would release them from the tension and trauma. For now, though, the rising heat kept them in separate knots, jabbering interminably, though fans intermingled as last minute bets were hurriedly made. Hindus from the East

Coast of Demerara and a few hundreds from Berbice, especially from the town and district of New Amsterdam and Port Mourant, raised their voices and shouted out the rural eminence of their coolie customs; they imagined fortunes to be made; Destiny would win! Yes, they argued, one to another, Swami Devan had brought Hinduism into the race. For a while, in the intense humidity of tropical South America, it seemed like a wholly new religion had been born, its centre no longer the ruminant cow, the creature suggestive of a placid heaven, but a horse, agile, graceful, pistons in its hooves, galloping into a mirage-like stasis and eating up the dirt at the same time, pulling the ground away from under its feet, clods of earth like huge stones flying behind it as it ran. Now, at any moment, this horse could take off from the ground, a flying pegasus. Hindus bawled out as the rhapsody of this image gripped their imagination, tormented them. Others argued that Destiny was a demon horse, a creature that was known to snort and rant unpredictably, flame coming out of its nostrils, fire in its eyes; a dragon of a horse. They had all heard the rumours. And what about the other horse? Don Dinero? It was less spirited, no? It was stable, controlled, economical in its strides, yet it too ate up the dirt, it too ran like... well, the devil?

For some it was simply a match race, but this mundane view didn't last for long.

And closer to the moment of the race, another view spread through the crowd. Destiny began to be seen as a bona-fide Guianese horse bred from the lush green grass of the mother-soil in the country of many waters, sugar-cane, rice, bauxite; this same coastland horse would match strides against that bred from the best thoroughbred strains in the Caribbean. Yes, Don Dinero, said the billboard, had raced in Trinidad, Barbados and Jamaica, and there was talk that it might have been sold to an Englishman so that it would race at Ascot in the United Kingdom, with the Queen Mother herself watching it with studied surprise, Lester Piggot, no less, aboard.

But this was quickly countered by an enterprising Hindu

who said that Mr. Bhairam's Destiny could easily be sold to an American to race at Churchill Downs and it could win the Kentucky Derby with all the additional vitamins it would receive according to true American training methods, and thereafter with Willie Shoemaker holding its reins... it could go on to win the Triple Crown! Yes, such a horse could be the sire of Northern Dancer.

The odds seemed to be on Don Dinero one moment, the next they reverted to Destiny; see-sawing like this for the best part of an hour, a race in itself. Speculation smouldered in an atmosphere reeking of rum, fanned from time to time by the trade winds bringing the pungency of crabs, molluscs, mullets across the sea-walls, and the scent of pure molasses from the Diamond Sugar Estate on the East Bank of Demerara, mixed as it was with the smell of sewage and rancid sugar-cane. But when the trade winds dropped, perfumes from the Indian women sitting on the main stand drifted faintly in a wan breeze, the imported smell of India mingling in the overall aroma of bodies, beings, presences. All this invigorated the men to talk more loudly; provoked those of darker hues to eye the supple brown-skinned women who custom had put beyond their reach and then to revert to the more voluptuous Georgetown bred. In this interplay of races, hybrid passions spirited out of subconscious minds in loud guffaws, the emptying of a collective mind.

Some began to say that because of the injury to Destiny's foot, it couldn't possibly win against a Trinidadian-bred horse, Don Dinero, fed on the actual pitch from the Pitch Lake in La Brea, whereas Mr. Bhairam's was merely fed on rice-pap. But another quickly countered that he had actually seen Destiny run at gallops, right here at D'Urban Park – like the wind. 'Only if he go be in form, man,' replied another, an African, for he too had seen Destiny run when it was trained by Jacob Athan. And where was Jacob Athan now? Well, he was with the Syndicate!

This spread like fresh news, causing another ripple, then a mammoth stir among a cluster of spectators on the main stand; and the heat brought out the vociferous and easily agitated into further claims and counterclaims. One voice rang out that it was because of Athan that Destiny had won the previous years. A woman of mixed race, kinky-haired but with pasty white skin, the hair like coiled black snakes ready to devour all-comers, cried out in half-jest, 'Is who does actually run de race, eh? Trainer or haas? Who does run wid four legs, eh? Gawd, Guyanese people does be stupid, eh! Look at dem arguin' over who does mek a haas run!' But another, more sedately, and lachrymose after he had knocked back a few glasses of rum with Jacob Athan's stable-hands, said that Athan could make even a jackass run like the wind if he set his mind to it, a real miracle-worker.

'What about Swami Devan, eh?'

'Yes – what about he?'

'He too could do dat!'

'Can he?'

'Yes, yes. He, a man of God.'

'Dat is Hindu god!'

'All gods de same. You ever hear he preach? Eh? Dat man is a orator, an' I hear it dat he can talk to a haas and mek it run.'

Another shouted, 'If Jacob Athan can mek a jackass run like de wind, Swami Devan can mek a cow fly higher than a crow. An' if he wants, he could mek dat same cow run faster than lightning an really jump over de moon!'

The track was hard-hard, said another, not even a demon horse could run fast on it; it would cause a horse's bones to crack, the legs to splinter like kindling. But this brought laughter from a fat-bodied woman who made her living selling plantains and bananas at the Stabroek Market, and she let out a clarion shout that a racehorse had bones like steel and no Guiana mud-ground could cause a thoroughbred animal to stumble and fall and dead. But a thoroughbred haas come from Araby, came the reply; it used to de desert, it got camel blood and dat's why Prince Aga Khan own de best of them. But what religion is he, eh? What religion, tell me dat, does this dude-

Prince belong to, came another raucous cry.

Gocolram, some distance away from the main pavilion where a number of All India League members and their families sat, took in the scene with a detached air, struggling to retain his serenity despite the swirling heat which seemed eager to suffocate everyone. Looking at the crowd, he wondered when last he'd seen D'Urban Park so packed and with so much excitement. He tried to imagine Hindus, Christians, Muslims in a temple, he imagined them singing bhajans in a loud, shrill voice; next they were all at a puja and sharing prasad, the blessed food, so sweetly cloying. No, it couldn't be, he told himself: it was too surreal a vision. Once more he looked up at the main stand for members of the All India League and thought he saw someone looking like Aurobindo Ghose. Was it really he? Next he thought he saw Mrs. Bhairam resplendent in a whitish sari, worn specially to deflect the heat, sensible woman that she was. But where was Mr. Bhairam? Gocolram's eyes roved the pavilion. No doubt Mr. Bhairam was keeping a close eye on his horses. Someone muttered almost in his ears, 'Destiny bound to develop foot trouble; the track too hard. Wait an' see.' Smiling approval, he turned around to greet the speaker, but there was only the sniff of rum in the air.

Almost at the opposite end of the main pavilion Devan was busily wiping perspiration from his face. The large crowd unsettled him and he wished he wasn't there. He laughed giddily and glanced at the seats on the pavilion, observing the members of the All India League, the ones he was able to recognise, some with binoculars, watching, eager, anxious. He dabbed more perspiration from his face, and wished he was one of them, looking through binoculars himself; he would keep a close watch on the behaviour of the youths, their every move, there were hundreds of them here. He looked around anxiously, a little terrified. Spectators jostled left and right, and Devan didn't care that no one recognised him in the anonymity of the heat, though he heard his name uttered like a shriek from time to time.

In the swirling haze he walked on alone, quickly. He

thought of Lall, Dr. Chu... was he a Hindu? He was Chinese. Impossible! Buddhist maybe. No, no, a Christian. Enemy! He wanted to see Lall, to find out just what Dr. Chu intended doing to Destiny. And then he noticed a familiar face. It was, wasn't it? That face, a youth's. Jotish? He called out his son's name, loudly, and peered, and called out again. 'Jotish, Jotish! Is it you, boy?' But his son, though only ten yards away from him, was flailing in the midst of a dense cluster of people. As Devan tried to fight his way in, someone recognised him and yelled out to him – he, the trainer of Destiny. Yes, Destiny would win! Win! Wouldn't it, Swami? Tell us, come on! Laughter. Sneers. And Devan felt goaded, he stretched out his hands, trying to force a way through.

'JOTISH!' he yelled. 'Is me, boy, you fadder! Don't you recognise me? Is me, Swami Devan.' He stopped suddenly as someone pulled his collar in recognition, and as he wrestled to be free, he wished again he was back in his room at the Villa: he didn't belong here. Yet, there was Jotish, there was no mistaking him. And now, instead of the Villa, memories of his room in Providence Village flooded back to him: the wooden floor with cracks, Jotish alongside him, eyes closed, they were both praying.

He was almost within reaching distance of the boy when an ocean of sounds announced that the race was on. Voices slapped against his ears; cries for Destiny and Don Dinero. The race was on!

More voices slapped against him, overwhelming his consciousness, hissing and swirling against his hearing.

'Son, son,' he called out, 'Jotish, can you hear me, boy? Come here!' He looked around instinctively now for Tara: she too had to be here; she would be close to the boy, wouldn't she? Half-veiled as she would appear in the heat, half-veiled, like a disguise... The race was on! Destiny against Don Dinero – the crowd cheering, jubilant one moment, ugly the next; calling out to one or other of the horses. Devan continued reaching for his son.

The boy indeed heard him now, and was making his way

closer. Devan stretched out another hand; shoulders, heads intervened. The cry went up, 'Don Dinero! The Syndicate! Don Dinero!' The words buffeted him, kept slapping him in his innermost recesses. Jotish was close by, their fingers touching, twirling; Jotish who used to collect hibiscus flowers for him and join him in his early morning rituals in Providence Village. They were close now Jotish looked taller, his face somewhat different, gaunt, darker too. 'Destiny go win! Destiny go win!' he heard, and he looked ahead at the track, but could see little, only hear their cries ringing in his head. Impulsively he urged, 'Hurry up, Jotish. Hurry up, boy!' The fingers, hands, warm together. 'I is here, Pa!' the boy answered, breathing hard.

Devan pulled his son closer to him, and the boy muttered, 'Me come fo' watch de race. Ma said you go be here. She right!'

'Where is she?'

But they were drowned out by more cries for Destiny; the horse was running into the homestretch of the nine-furlong race, and Devan sensed it: as if the horse, in the frenzy of his mind, was running across the entire country, starting with Providence Village, then Tarlogie on the Corentyne, next Mahaica and ending up in Georgetown, the horse now pulling away, with extraordinary power, pulling away still, by three, four, five, six lengths! Mr. Bhairam was leaping off his feet on the main stand, and Mrs. Bhairam cried tears of sweet joy. Devan throbbed as he held on to his son in the maelstrom of the excitement; the boy looked up at him in the fullness of recognition, without a tincture of surprise.

A lull, like a yawning silence – but for a moment only; then someone cried out, 'De haas gone wild!' Others picked up the words, it became a collective chant, an incantation: 'Wild, wild, de haas gone wild! Wild, wild, de haas gone wild! Destiny gone crazy!' Devan held on more tightly to Jotish in the midst of the pandemonium, and urged, 'Come on, we mus' get outa here, now!'

But me come fo' see de race, Pa,' Jotish protested.

'Now!' Devan ordered, asserting paternal authority, and he wondered if the boy had indeed turned into a rascal.

A further roar from the crowd, and when someone said the jockey on Destiny had fallen because he could no longer control the horse, Devan shook his head in silent agony. There was a blur in his mind's eye. Was it really the heat causing this sensation? He felt the tug of his son's hand against his arm, bringing him back to the present, into focus. 'Me want to see, Pa. Fo' see the haas! Destiny, Pa!' Devan looked at Jotish remonstratively, regretfully; his mind blurred, the sensation overpowering, and he knew he must reach the northern exit before it was too late; before the crowd became a scrimmage, a riot of disappointed hopes: the pandemonium breaking out in earnest. 'Hare Krishna, Hare Ram,' he let out, and his son, watching him, grimaced.

And yet another resounding cry: 'De jockey fall down! Destiny gone wild! Look, an ambulance comin' fo' pick up de boy!' The heat was suffocating, and Devan wished it would rain; yet he also wanted to see if Destiny had indeed gone wild. What had Dr. Chu done to the horse? Maybe Lall would tell him. 'Hare Ram,' he muttered, looking around, seeing faces, eyes all looking at him, in the giant swirl, all accusing him.

Aggressively, as if he couldn't stand any more of it, he pushed his way to reach the exit; and Jotish, emboldened by his father, kicked at someone in the way, sucking his teeth, aggressively. Again Devan wondered about the boy. But he also wanted to know if Punam was seriously hurt, if Destiny was hurt, and he looked back... Closer to the exit now, who could he ask? Who? Instead he looked at Jotish and asked, 'Where is yuh ma?'

There was no answer, for a more distant cry came to his ears, like the echo of a recent event, all too familiar, all too near; it had been foreboding and now was real. 'Destiny been doped! Doped? Yes, doped!' Suddenly Devan felt like laughing because he imagined Lall's frantic expression, his urge to scurry away, and he laughed out loud. Jotish looked up at him, grimaced once more, and said, 'Ma waitin' fo' you in Enmore.'

'What?'

'Ma—'

'Never mind she now, son,' he blurted out, as he passed the exit; he was outside, but not before thinking of the All India League once more, he had reached the exit of that too. 'Doped! Doped!' he heard the cry ringing out, a clarion of distress. And Jotish said, 'We come fo' see de race, Pa. De race!'

'Never mind dat, it all over.'

Jotish bore a look of deep disappointment on his face, he was on the verge of tears: he thought of running away, freeing himself from his father and getting lost in the crowd, but the noise, the pandemonium, terrified him, and he merely held on more tightly to his father's thumb as he led the way. But Devan, though breathing in cleaner air away from the crowd, nevertheless felt a whirring in him, like a thousand bees following, chasing after him, stinging him, from inside, outside, there was no place really to escape. 'Hare Ram,' he said once more, inaudibly, following his son, out, far out.

Mr. Bhairam, with a tragic expression, more tragic than anyone had ever seen, muttered: 'I can't believe all this! I can't!' Mrs. Bhairam endlessly wiped tears away with her sari and leant close to her husband, as she hadn't done in a long time, and watched the awe-struck crowd round Destiny: the horse foaming at the mouth and lying on the ground as if it would die at any moment. A number of other Hindus loudly commiserated, 'Is true Swami Devan dope the haas?' Again Mr. Bhairam muttered, 'I can't believe this; no, I can't.' And someone else said, 'You shouldn't have trusted him.'

Bhairam turned round, not sure who the speaker was, until he caught sight of Gocolram's smiling face, and Lall's nearby. Lall came closer, though not with his usual scurrying intensity, and said, 'But where is he, eh?' Mrs. Bhairam wiped more tears from her face, her eyes roving the crowd for the one she'd always trusted, her eyes fiery red. And there were more tears, as of a greater sorrow.

When Sarwan Singh, in gentleman's fashion, came to commiserate, Mr. Bhairam muttered more loudly, 'I can't believe all this.' And Singh, in a dry tone, said, 'Of course, your horse will be disqualified. The evidence is very clear. All members of the League have seen for themselves.' With a solemn face masking his joy, he walked away, quickly.

Lall, with a marked pout which made his face distinctly narrow – like an agouti's – and looking particularly at Gocolram, said to Mr. Bhairam, 'You should never trust rural Hindus, Bhai. Swami Devan, remember, is from... ' But Bhairam wasn't listening; he was looking at his horse and moaning as if he was witnessing a deeply personal death. Inwardly he longed to get back to his harmonium, to seek out its reclusive harmonies.

The East Coast train chug-chugged along, the heavy jangle of iron and steel and chains rattling, so distinctive a sound in British Guiana. For a time it kept Devan alert as he watched the coastland forests suddenly converge, then retreat as the train hurtled on its way. Where the thick brush was missing, houses on stilts appeared, some leaning at an angle, and it seemed to Devan as if the land was moving, the train still, houses on stilts running away. Then, it was as if the train was leaning on a precipice and he was on a journey in a foreign land; it wasn't Guiana anymore. Banana leaves grazed his face, whipping by, and not far behind the last group of houses he saw a cluster of very tall coconut trees, some like bent old men, about to fall resoundingly to the ground. Devan closed his eyes, trying not to think about anything in particular... but it was a younger Jotish he saw, gathering hibiscus flowers, and he patting him on the head as he sat and crossed his legs, close to him in his familiar room in Providence Village; they were burning incense and meditating. He was about to reach out to pat the boy's head in his reverie, when a louder clang of iron and steel brought him back to the present. Pulling back his hand, he thought of the boy's future.

And just when Jotish thought his father had dozed off, he heard him say: 'You mustn' tell you ma what you see today.'

'Eh?'

'You ma–'

'Why not?'

Devan opened his eyes wide. 'Don't ask dat question!' he snapped, lifting himself up a little, again wondering if the boy had become a rascal. Then, under his breath he muttered, 'Haas is not part of me destiny.' He closed his eyes once more, tightly this time; but a few seconds later he opened them again and asked, 'Tell me, Jotish, you turn rascil?'

'Rascil?'

'Yes-yes.'

'Me na understand.' The boy looked puzzled, then sucked his teeth, the sound rising above the clang of iron and steel.

Devan merely eyed him, father at son, stranger at stranger, and he replied, 'Never mind.' And again he tried meditating, this time reflecting on ethics, on Gandhi's *Art of Living*: how he enjoyed that book. Before long he felt serene, and a little later he put out a hand, touching Jotish. As if this was a cue, Jotish let out:

'Wake up! We reach!'

'What? Where?' Devan rubbed his eyes and swallowed hard, not without anxiety.

'Enmore.'

'Where's Tara?' He rubbed his eyes again, wide awake. Jotish pointed to the platform as the train started pulling up. For a moment Devan couldn't focus clearly and again he rubbed his eyes, and he wondered if he was really still dreaming. Then he remembered what had crossed his mind while the train lulled him into sleep, amid the clang of iron and steel: cows, sheer cows in his life, the cows he'd been promised on his wedding day. 'Cows indeed,' he muttered under his breath. Then he looked ahead, at Jotish running forward.

Then he saw Tara, hands akimbo, on the platform; and the platform seemed to be moving, just a little, away from him.

Could Tara be leaving, really? Then he saw his daughters, Shanti and Devi, close to their mother: they too had their hands akimbo, all waiting for him to join them. But the platform refused to remain still, and Devan felt a dire fear of losing them forever.

Jotish looked at him, pointed, and laughed hard – and gleefully.

Cyril Dabydeen was born in the Canje district in Guyana, South America. His grandfather, popularly known as 'Albion Driver', moved to the Rose Hall sugar estate where Dabydeen grew up and attended, and later taught at, the St. Patrick's Anglican school. He finished his formal education at Queen's University in Canada. He has done an assortment of work, but mainly taught at Algonquin College and at the University of Ottawa. He has published widely in small magazines in Canada and abroad. His books of poetry include: *Poems in Recession* (1972), *Distances* (1977), *Goatsong* (1977), *Heart's Frame* (1979), *This Planet Earth* (1979), *Still Close to the Island* (1980), *Elephants Make Good Stepladders* (1982), *Islands Lovelier Than A Vision* (1986) and *Coastland* (1989). He has published two collections of short stories, *Still Close to the Island* (1980) and *To Monkey Jungle* (1988) and one novel, *Dark Swirl* (1989).